Praise for other Magic Carpet Erotic Romances...

A Brush With Love by Maria Isabel Pita

Ms. Pita once again entrances the reader with the flowing melody of her words, the detailed and intriguing characters, and the passionate demonstration of love and submission freely given. Miranda is a confident woman, who loves her life and embraces it while seeking more from it. Michael is confident and so incredibly sexy. He looks for nothing beyond his art and within it he finds the beautiful Miranda. His pursuit is relentless and he desires to please her with dominance and finds that it fits his powerful, confident, quiet persona. Their love affair touches quick at the soul. The sex had me wishing for an entire new set of toys. The passion is a blazing inferno of lust, love, and surrender for all involved. This is a story that must not be missed.

—*Just Erotic Romance Reviews*

Secret Desires – Two Erotic Romances by Frances LaGatta & Laura Muir

Is it possible to write a romance novel that is also HOT? If you don't think so, then you've never read anything by LaGatta and Muir. These two gals know how to turn up the heat in writing that is descriptive, dreamy, romantic and lyrical, while sparkling with sexual encounters that are powerfully erotic. LaGatta's style is sensual in the classic sense: all the senses are engaged here, the reader made super-aware of the sights and smells and sounds that provide the backdrop for primitive sex in the lush jungles of

Peru. Laura Muir's trip is to closer, more intimate places – the dreams of the poet intrude on reality, and the joy of discovering love is sent to greater heights by the power of sexual seduction and conquest. If you like Romance novels and if you like your sex hot and steamy, then Secret Desires is the place for you.

—*Don Winslow*

Cat's Collar – Three Erotic Romances
by Maria Isabel Pita

Women have many fantasies, linked by common themes, and these three wonderfully erotic tales seem to have captured them all. In "Dreams of Anubis", you will, like Mary Fallon, quickly slip away from the humdrum of the office to travel back and forth between modern Egypt and the old Kingdoms, seeking only new knowledge and your true love. You feel the sand slipping between your toes and the hot wind on your face as you make your way to the mysteries of Imhotep, filled by the pleasures of incredible sexual dreams and hot sex. Do you do as Simon says or as his nemesis, Sir Richard Ashley, desires?

In "Rituals of Surrender", you join Maia Wilson, struck by lightening near an ancient oak in a Druid forest, lingering between different worlds. Caught like a fly in a carefully planned web of intrigue and magic, you need to choose your lover. Will you stay with Chris and his incredible tree house or be pulled into the comfort of Drew Landson's black leather jacket. What will your mother say?

In "Cat's Collar", with the flick of a whip, you find yourself, like Mira Rosemond, wanting to please your Master, Phillip, as he introduces you to new pleasures in his secret bondage "playroom" by his wine cellar. See what the cat brought home!

If you have not read Maria Isabel Pita before, you will be amazed by her wit, her incredible knowledge, both arcane and sensual, and her exquisite attention to detail. If you are a fan of hers already, you will continue to appreciate the artistry of her work and your only disappointment will be when the stories end and you have to move back into your own skin. Like Mira, pour yourself a nice glass of wine in a crystal glass and savor the experience and say, "Oh, yes… Master!" —*The Romance Studio*

DREAMS OF ANUBIS, RITUALS OF SURRENDER and CAT'S COLLAR should be classified as cerebral erotica. None of them are 'fluff' or 'light fiction', but rather they force the reader to be actively thinking while reading to grasp their high concepts and complexities… You feel truly satisfied with the journeys you read, and in many ways are a part of. All three books share a commonality in which each heroine is torn between difficult choices she has to make. In the first two stories, the heroines have metaphysical paths that they must traverse that lead them to happiness and their soul mates. These stories do an excellent job of integrating faith, trust, and what is real versus the surreal. The third story is more of a contemporary erotic romance detailing the course the heroine must choose to be with the man she loves and understand the Master/slave roles they live. Each novel has many erotic scenes that are enmeshed with the plot – to give up the tangible and trust body and soul to another is what defines the erotic in Cat's Collar. —*Cupid's Library Reviews*

Mutual Holdings by Susan DiPlacido

Ms. DiPlacido is a thoroughly seasoned author, and it shines through with this outstandingly written book. Ms. DiPlacido lets Lisa do the talking, and what a talker Lisa is. She relates her tale of confused and frustrated love, leaving the reader in stitches. Lisa's dry humor is biting at times. You will come away from this story feeling like a friendship has developed, the closeness only a good writer can achieve and deliver to its fullest degree. The only thing you might not like about this book is your inability to put it down.

—Road to Romance

Whispered Secrets by Terri Pray

I thoroughly enjoyed reading Whispered Secrets with such an independent and confident heroine who knows what she wants out of life, and in her bedroom. Ms. Pray does an excellent job of keeping the momentum of the story alive without boring her readers. Whispered Secrets touches on some modern day dating dilemmas and the issues single women face in relationships. The characters are... real people you can associate with; especially seeing them grow as individuals through the love, trust and faith they discover in each other. This contemporary tale of the love Kate unexpectedly discovers with Frank is gratifying and ends on a high note. I would recommend Whispered Secrets for anyone who is interested in contemporary erotic romance.

—Just Erotic Romance Reviews

Guilty Pleasures by Maria Isabel Pita

Guilty Pleasures explores the passionate willingness of women throughout the ages to offer themselves up to the forces of love. Historical facts are seamlessly woven into graphic sexual encounters. Pita does indeed take us through the ages, from the near-future time of 2015 A.D., back through the 20th century, then the 19th, 18th, 17th, 16th, 15th, 12th centuries, back to 1000 B.C., 3000 B.C., through to another solar system, and on to a parallel universe. What will amaze you, if not even alarm you, is Pita's eye for detail and her uncanny feel for the everyday lives of her distant characters. When you read her stories of ancient lovers, for example, you will believe that Pita herself has visited those times and is merely recounting to you first-hand what she observed, endured, and felt while she was there. In these pages, Pita's unique imagination is unleashed and she spares no punches. I guarantee that you will marvel at the complexity of the places she takes you to and what her characters learn there. Guilty Pleasures is an absolute must for any fan of literary erotica.

—*Marilyn Jaye Lewis*

Maria Isabel Pita takes us through a collection of 18 erotic stories which capture the enthusiasm and passion of different women throughout the ages, with astounding precision. The author displays an unusual, albeit ingenious, imagination that opens the book with **Out of Control**, a short story set in futuristic Canada 2015... It's difficult to suggest favourites as I enjoyed them all... with each tale comes a new premise, amalgamated with historical facts and wonderful, descriptive exposition. Every character is written with a fresh, unique outlook on love and life appropriate to the chosen historical era. This fact alone hooked me from the first sentence, or at least the opening paragraph of each story. *Ms Pita* varies the pace of her writing, in a well-planned effort to intrigue and arouse the reader. All in all, *Maria's* ability to mix the erotic pursuits of her characters with entertaining, sometimes shocking twists and turns, ensures a believable, dynamic ending to each self-contained story. These stories capture a mixture of cruel, sensual overriding power, and exotic scenes; intensifying the creative suspense of an exhilarating read not to be missed.

—*Women's Fiction Reviews*

The Fire in Starlight

by

Maria Isabel Pita

First Magic Carpet Books, Inc. edition June 2006

Published in 2006

Manufactured in the United States of America
Published by Magic Carpet Books, Inc.

Magic Carpet Books, Inc.
PO Box 473
New Milford, CT 06776

Library of Congress Cataloging in Publication Date

The Fire in Starlight
Maria Isabel Pita

ISBN: 0-9774311-2-6

Book Design: P. Ruggieri

Dedication

For my love, and our secret forest,
which just keeps deepening and growing...

Prologue

Seven years of her life gone, wasted... but that's not true, she was doing a lot more with her time than just being in love with a person she never wants to see again. How these things happen is a mystery millions of men and women have pondered throughout the ages, yet Sofia always believed herself magically immune to such protracted catastrophes. She scarcely noticed the mileage accumulating, the years flowing by before the crash, when she suddenly realized the promising love she had wholeheartedly bought into had degenerated into a routine shell not worth fixing. Towards the end they had sex less and less, but when they did she could somehow make herself forget she had been forced to schedule their lovemaking like an oil change. Afterwards, she was relaxed enough not to think about how unsatisfied she was with so many aspects of her lover apart from his big hard cock. She was the one with all the secret fantasies, he simply provided the erection she writhed around lost in a daydream, her eyes closed and her soul somewhere else – with *someone* else – entirely. She thought perhaps this was the way of things – that beginnings were always more passionate and inspired – and that she was wrong to continue desiring so much more. She strove to behave like a responsible adult, applying rational band aids to the frustrations she treated like paper cuts, painful but inevitable in the real world where life was much easier if you split the bills. Sofia had not believed herself capable of such denial, but she was now faced with the evidence of how, for far too long, she had murdered her deepest feelings in the name of love in order to remain comfortable; to preserve an illusion of satisfaction and safety. It was appalling how clearly she saw herself abruptly, as though for years her reflective soul had been fogged by steamy sex, and in the end she was left alone staring at her lovely face in disgusted wonder that she had proved to be just another vulnerably confused woman after all.

But that was all behind her now, that bumpy seven-year-long road was history in her mental rearview mirror. Amazingly enough, it took only seven days to drive away from seven years, and since then she had grown (positively blossomed) inside in subtle ways that transported her light years beyond the cowardly, compromising Sofia she had allowed herself to become. The actual road she was cruising down was smooth, freshly paved and painted by the look of it – Highway 956 taking her through Ethel into Clinton. It was late in the day on the ninth of February and she was glad of the brand new reflectors on the central yellow line that helped illuminate the pitch-black asphalt because there were no street-lights this far away from the city. She was only forty-five minutes from her old apartment home in Baton Rouge, but already she was in another world. She had lived in BR all her life, and yet she had never ventured this far north before. The LSU campus had been her universe for over fifteen years, a purple and gold cocoon ripped open by two hurricanes of loss – her relationship ending, and her best friend and colleague dying, both on the same night. The very evening she and Steve were arguing, and his arm suddenly shot out to push her away, dear sweet Robert was clutching his left arm in his lakeside home and dying alone. The symmetry was sinister; uncanny. Perhaps at the exact moment she was stunned to discover herself lying in the bathtub her old friend was falling in the shower, and in her mind she shared the pain of his heart attack the instant she realized her life as she knew it was over. Robert's life as he knew it was also over forever, but she fervently hoped he had moved on to a better, more fulfilling state of being, just as she was striving to do now driving to the house he had unexpectedly left her in his Will.

Robert was the old, steady limb on which her introverted cocoon had hung throughout the years. First he was her professor, and without him she never would have gotten through her dissertation, then finally they were colleagues and best friends. In retrospect, it was his intellectual and emotional companionship that had made it possible for her to mask the problems with her relationship. On campus she always had someone to talk to, to share her every thought and feeling with, so that when she went home in the evenings she didn't miss this intimacy as much she otherwise would have; as much as she should have. She went home to be comfortable and to have sex, in that order. Steve often greeted her with a Vodka Martini in hand, a delectable assortment of deli meats and cheeses artfully arranged on a platter waiting for them on a table in front of the television. Alcohol and COX Cable helped distract her from how little she had in common with her boyfriend besides the monthly bills and the weekend fucks, during which she sought to exorcise the beautiful demons of her fantasies, which sadly melted away on Monday mornings like vampires done to death by the stake of unchanging routine. Cable TV was like a fly with hundreds of eyes showing the same things all the time, an increasingly annoying, deathless buzz in her head when she was trying to sleep and Steve stayed up channel surfing every single night of the week. She could count on one hand the programs she liked to watch, and it was a source of perverse satisfaction to her now that in Clinton she would be lucky to get any reception at all.

Sabbatical... such a sweet word. It was all hers, for over a year, maybe for two if she could stretch her savings, and she was determined to. Sofia was very glad now that she and Steve had never even entertained the thought of a joint bank account. At the time she hadn't realized how meaningful it was that she had no desire to merge all her assets with his, yet now it struck her as an obvious symbol of how much she was holding back, and of the fact that she didn't truly trust him. It could be said he had stolen some of the best years of her life, but the truth was she had given them away freely and had only herself to blame for their loss, really. She had always known he had a violent temper he managed to keep under control with her, but he had never once hit her until that night when she ended up in the bathtub, the shower curtain crumpled beneath her helping to break her fall.

The bruises had faded, but for days they served as reminders she was doing the right thing by leaving him. And yet if Robert hadn't passed away and given her a place to stay, would she have been able to so quickly and single-mindedly pack all the stuff she had bought with her salary and credit cards, and in seven short days abandon the man she had theoretically loved for seven long years? There was no point asking such a question; circumstances, and her response to them, told her in no uncertain terms that she needed not only to define but to defend her thoughts and feelings with a boldness she had never had the courage to exercise before. Steve was an atheist, and even though she hadn't been to church since she was a little girl, she had never lost her faith in *something*. It was high time she did some serious soul searching to figure out exactly what it was she believed. She had the time and the space now, she was free of students and boyfriends and all responsibilities except to herself.

The first decision Sofia made was that she definitely did *not* believe in chance or coincidence. Too many times the experiences of her life seemed choreographed to get her to move in a certain direction, and these last dramatic events felt like a cosmic slap in the face. She never would have imagined twenty acres of land in Clinton, LA were part of her fate, but they suddenly were, and she was grateful that, in a sense, Robert would still be with her while she was feeling more alone than ever.

After consulting the directions printed out for her by the attorney, Sofia took a right turn at a crossroads. The setting sun's golden-red head appeared in the rearview mirror, encouraging her with its beautiful intensity to defy the sedate speed limit and accelerate due east towards a new beginning.

Chapter One

I t was a race against the darkness. Sofia cursed herself for not having left the city earlier in the day. The fact that circumstances had been beyond her control seemed a lame excuse now as the absence of traffic fortunately allowed her to switch on her high beams. On the other hand, being completely alone on the road made her nervous, and intensely grateful for the two luminous swords defending her, even though it was a relief to sheathe them for a few seconds when she saw another car heading her way. It had taken her less than three minutes to drive through the quaint old town of Clinton. Vaguely, she recalled reading somewhere that there was a local farmer's market in front of the historic courthouse every first Saturday of the month. She slowed down to obey the speed limit, and took note of several little antique shops, consoling herself with this evidence that she had not left civilization completely behind. The city felt much farther away than it actually was, as if it was on the other side of a black hole opening up onto another universe the darker it got and the farther she drove. Dusk in Baton Rouge had threatened her with nothing more than terrible traffic, statistically more dangerous than lonely country roads, yet paradoxically she had felt safer on I-10 than she did in what, to her, felt like the middle of nowhere.

The moving company had been three hours late, and tried to make up for it by carting away her boxes, and the few pieces of furniture she had decided to keep, with breakneck speed. Her back increasingly tense from the stress of making sure they didn't accidentally load any of Steve's stuff into the truck, Sofia was glad she didn't have time to linger sentimentally in the comfortable *Jefferson Place* apartment she had shared with him for so long. She was almost late for her appointment with Robert's attorney. He was surprisingly young, and coolly indifferent in a powder-blue suit as he informed her the house was only minimally furnished, so there would be plenty of room for her own things. The utilities had been turned on and switched over into her name, and a cleaning crew had been there yesterday. She could move in right away. The Deed to the property was in her briefcase, the incredible fact that she was now both a house and a land owner spelled out in neat black-and-white on 8 x 10 paper, nevertheless, the lawyer's glib Southern twang pronouncing, "It's not too far, just a few miles north of Clinton, is all" had been completely misleading. She was not prepared for the visceral vastness of the country; for the sense of profound distances winding themselves through her gut as she followed the serpentine curves of increasingly darker and narrower roads. The silhouettes of trees were sharply drawn against a hauntingly pale, almost silver sky. The sun had set, but the day was taking a blessedly long time to die. The glowing blue displays on her dashboard as she kept anxious track of the passing miles had never looked more beautiful. Her car kept the atmosphere of civilization reassuringly around her, and she was more grateful than ever for its reliable comfort.

The house Robert had built for his family so long ago couldn't be far now; it was located somewhere in this endless landscape of rolling pastures and trees. Every now and then her headlights washed over a mailbox and she glimpsed the crouching shape of a house warm with lights burning inside it that kept her hope alive. Then at long last she came to her street – Rosalyn Lane. She took a left turn onto a purported dirt road actually covered with gravel that made a raucous banging, pinging symphony beneath her crunching tires that had her fearing for the insides of her *Mitsubishi*. The distant surreal silhouettes of cows eternally grazing disappeared as she found herself surrounded by trees, and she realized with a stab of disbelief that all the naked limbs caressed by her high beams belonged to her. Here and there the jade-green gleam of Magnolia leaves relieved the starkness, rooting the wintry scene in the Deep South where it hardly ever snowed and where it was never cold long enough to pain the soul.

She slowed down when a mailbox leapt into her headlights. 3610 was painted by a steady hand in glowing white numbers on the black metal. She was here, she had made it, and she was so happy and relieved she cried out in triumph at finding what, at that moment, felt like her own personal Holy Grail. Right on cue, her stomach grumbled. It's all about *surviving*, hunger reminded her, deepening the pleasure she took in this landmark moment as she thought about the big cooler in her trunk filled with cheeses, cold cuts, and bread – the bare essentials she needed to live until she did her first grocery shopping. And of course she had also brought two cases of wine with her, one red and one white.

With reverent slowness she turned into the driveway of her new home, following a winding path between the trees. A structure loomed to her left, but she lost sight of it as she was forced to do an almost 360° turn. Then there it was, directly before her at last, a real, solid house, her headlights making the windows look even more unwelcomingly dark.

Sofia did not turn off the engine right away. She rested her head back against the seat. "Oh Robert, Robert!" she murmured. "I'm sorry… thank you!" A deepening sense of shame overruled even her hunger pains. She had a Ph.D. in obscure folk poetry, verses written where nights were as impenetrably black as the one pressing against the technological shell of her car, but always she had read these silent songs in rooms lit up by electricity. It filled her with a humbling awe to suddenly realize Robert had always known that, one day, she would be forced to face what she most loved along with all the things she most feared. However, she had more than enough time to begin deconstructing herself tomorrow, at the moment she was avoiding the scary thrill of walking alone into a dark house that had been empty for years but that was now all hers to do with as she willed.

Thankfully there was a flashlight under her seat, a weapon she could use even though its light was powerless against subconscious shadows and all the irrational fears they inspired. She told herself very firmly that there was no one hiding in the house waiting to attack her. The cleaning crew had been there yesterday and locked the doors behind them; she was perfectly safe. She shut off the engine and the lights and got out of the car, and the first thing she noticed were the stars, followed a close second by the half moon hanging directly above the black pyramid of the roof. The beauty of the sky was a shocking surprise. She had lived in the city all her life and had never seen so many stars. She didn't turn on the flashlight, because with her head thrown back she felt absolutely no threat emanating from the darkness. Intellectually she had always understood fewer stars were visible than ever as a result of light pollution, but she wondered now how she could possibly have lived for so long with that sickly yellow glow above her instead of what she was seeing now. Right away she recognized Orion's belt, the universe casually slapping her with it and reprimanding her for not recognizing any other constellations. It was a cold night, the atmosphere was crystal clear, and how many stars she could see wasn't just a beautiful sight, it also mysteriously lifted her spirits. The flashlight in her hand which had felt so vital just a minute ago was forgotten as she made a 180° turn. When she faced away from the moon the stars became even more profuse, adorning the highest branches of trees like Christmas lights that never got turned off and stored in a dusty attic.

Reluctantly, Sofia lowered her gaze back down to earth and the exciting challenge before her. She flicked on the flashlight and shone it's beam across wooden steps leading up to the front door. She walked slowly, savoring the anticipation. She slipped her car keys into the pocket of her jacket, exchanging them for her new house keys as she noted with pleasure how big the porch was, stretching the whole length of the house. There were more windows than there were solid walls, and double French doors. From inside she would be able to see the woods stretching all around her.

She slipped the key in the lock and it turned smoothly. She held her breath as she crossed the threshold, scanning the walls on either side of her for a light switch. She found one, and flicked it up just as the door closed from its own weight behind her with a *click*! that echoed significantly while she and the house felt each other for the first time.

"Oh my!" she breathed. The walls were a forest-green that looked almost black at night beneath two atmospherically dim track lights set high in the walls on either side of a large, open space. Already she could tell that on lush summer days the house would seem to dissolve, blending with the foliage outside. She turned the circular knob next to the light switch clockwise, flooding the room with light. To her right was a rectangular dining room table that looked as if it had been fashioned from the bark of a single fallen tree, and six chairs that were equally rustic-looking and beautiful, their hardwood seats softened by violet cushions embroidered with green vines sprouting tiny red flowers. The rest of the room was empty except for a red, black and beige Oriental rug that covered a good portion of the polished wooden floorboards.

She was drawn to a narrow archway on the left side of the room and tried to find a light switch beyond it, but there didn't appear to be one. She swung the beam of the flashlight back and forth in growing amazement, scarcely daring to believe what she saw – a library, study and sitting room all in one. She had never seen this room before and yet her soul seemed to recognize it because she felt immediately at home. She saw a small stone fireplace, and on the left side of the room floor-to-ceiling shelves were already half filled with books Robert had left her. There were two windows on either side of the hearth, and a very comfortable looking green chair flanked by a round wooden table. On the other side of the room she made out a simple wooden desk beside which sat a modern computer stand.

"Oh Robert, this is beautiful! It's perfect!" She spoke out loud as though he was standing right behind her. To the left of the fireplace there was a neat stack of firewood as tall as she was, but the walls directly to the right and left of the archway were bare palettes. Already she could picture her loveseat in here, as well as a fold-out table she would buy right away so she could dine by firelight every night until Spring.

Sofia somehow tore herself away from this cozy alcove and made her way through the larger, echoing room. The kitchen was perfect for a person who enjoyed cooking. There was plenty of black Formica counter space, wooden cabinets with glass doors, and a black side-by-side refrigerator that looked brand-new. She was incredulous at the trouble Robert had apparently taken to make sure the house was made ready for her the minute he passed away. There seemed to be nothing he hadn't thought of, but that wasn't surprising; his sensitive attention to detail was one of the many things she had loved about him.

The bathroom was dominated by an old-fashioned tub with lion's paws completely surrounded by a glimmering blue shower curtain evocative of a waterfall against the large, clay-brown floor tiles. The counter and the sink were black marble beautifully contrasted by blonde wooden cabinets.

Two bedrooms opened up off the bathroom, and the largest one was absolutely empty. It must have been where Robert and his wife would have slept so long ago, and hers was to be the room never occupied by Rose, who was only four-years-old when she was killed with her mother on some cursed road. Sofia had brought blankets and pillows and an air bed to tide her over until the movers arrived in the morning, so she gasped with astonished pleasure when she saw that Robert had had other plans for her.

If it hadn't been for the modern ceiling fan and the four glass, tulip-shaped lights that bloomed to life when she flicked up the switch, she would have believed herself suddenly transported into another century. A massive bed dominated the smaller bedroom, flanked on both sides by two simple wooden nightstands. Yet no such bed could ever have existed in any actual past; it was a fairytale bed, a dream in itself. *Sleeping Beauty of the Woods*, she thought, designed to please a little girl's innocently passionate imagination. This was Aurora's bed, the one she lad flung herself across, weeping, when the three good fairies told her she could never again see the handsome young man she had met in the woods that afternoon. A simple rough-hewn wooden frame supported a mattress that looked impossibly delicious beneath a plush blue-green feather comforter decorated with a diamond pattern that was matched by two over-sized pillows, around which deep-blue velvet folds hung with heavy sensuality from an invisible frame.

"Oh *my* God!" she whispered. The unbelievably gorgeous bed would mysteriously comfort her when she cried herself to sleep at night, and inspire her to dream of a future where all her desires would be fulfilled by the man destined to be her prince...

There was something resting on one of the nightstands.

She quickly set the flashlight down and picked up an expensive vanilla-white sheet of paper folded neatly in half. Seating herself on the edge of the bed, she opened it slowly, unconsciously holding her breath...

My Dear Sofia,

The fact that you are reading this means I have moved on, but please do not grieve for me. I am happily sailing invisible waves of energy to another world and your tears will only drown me in a time and place I would have left long ago if it wasn't for you, my darling girl. As you must know, you were as beloved to me as the daughter I lost so long ago. I built this house for her. It has stood empty all these years because after Rose and her mother were killed I could not bear to set foot in it, yet I could not bear to sell it, either, and after I met you, I was very glad I had kept it. Almost from the moment we met, I knew this place was destined to be yours, Sofia. I suspected (I very much hoped) you would need it one day when you realized you had not yet met the man you deserve. I cannot imagine Steve burying himself in the country, but even if you're still together, the land and house will always belong only

to you. I pray you will love it there. Never doubt that we'll laugh and talk togeth-
er again, Sofia, but not for a long while, I hope. You are young and beautiful, in
every sense, and I insist that you live a long and happy life. That's the last assign-
ment I will give you, and I am confident you will do a beautiful job will all the years
you have to work with. I love you, dear.

Until later,
Robert

Slowly, reverently, she set the paper back down on the nightstand, and then a storm of weeping overwhelmed her, there was no other way to describe it. For an indeterminate amount of time she sat on the edge of the bed with her head in her hands feeling as though she was sobbing the soul right out of her body. When it became hard to breathe she stared up the ceiling, her chest heaving and tears streaming down her face making her flushed cheeks even hotter as they trickled onto her tongue like drops of holy water. Her tears tasted bitter-sweet indeed as she felt mysteriously blessed by the love creating them, the pain in her heart wordlessly praying that one day she would see her beloved friend again. People like Steve believed that when you died you were gone forever, but she knew in her heart that was impossible.

She picked up the letter again and pressed it fervently against her heart with both hands. "I love you Robert!" she declared passionately, her voice hoarse from sobbing. "I love you!"

Chapter Two

Her soul fortified by the mysterious endorphins of love and grief, Sofia's body reminded her in no uncertain terms that it was hungrier than ever now. She had a lot of hard, engrossing work ahead of her setting up her new home, and she was very thankful for that. It was still too painful to think clearly with memories buffeting her from every side of her psyche – images of her life for the last fifteen years crashing in colorful waves behind her visual cortex, moments wrought with irresistible emotional currents, and the undertows of subconscious doubts and fears that for years pulled her under and made it impossible for her to escape a relationship that was going nowhere. The love she and Steve had once truly shared, before it gradually evaporated into thin air, was an empty shell echoing in her soul. She wondered how long she would be haunted by her past as she kept seeing Robert, sitting behind the inspired chaos of his desk, smiling up at her with his darkly sober eyes. She was beginning to understand what he had thought about her and her love-life. She suspected that his sadness had sprung not only from his personal losses but also from witnessing her unhappiness – which she stubbornly denied – as she wasted herself living with the wrong man.

She turned on the outside lights and the porch was revealed like an empty stage by four spotlights, two on either side of the house, angled away from each other to illuminate bare trees and shrubs, and just enough of the gravel drive to enable her to unpack her trunk without fumbling in the dark. She began with the cooler of food, followed by the two boxes of wine. Her suitcase, her bathroom bag, and three miscellaneous boxes came last. Mentally she thanked Robert for her splendid new refrigerator, which looked even bigger when she filled it with everything she had brought and barely dented all its pristine storage space. The day after tomorrow, she decided, she would drive into Zachary and do some serious shopping. It was something to look forward to because she loved to dine well every night if she could, and she was relishing the thought of eating alone again. Steve hated vegetables and abhorred all seafood, whereas she was an avid omnivore. It was a small consolation for all she had lost that her culinary desires would no longer be restricted by the limited horizons of his palate.

She unpacked her two emergency wine glasses, rinsed out the smaller one, and filled it with her favorite California Chardonnay, still cold from the cooler. It dawned on her then with a sensation of pleasant satisfaction that she didn't really miss Steve at all. It was more the idea of how much time she had wasted with him that hurt so much. The reality of being by herself, away from everything she was consciously fully beginning to realize she had disliked about him, was actually quite pleasant, and invigorating.

It was cold in the house. She kept her jacket on as she searched for the central heat and air conditioning controls. It took her quite a while to program the little white box, but at last she heard a gas furnace kick in somewhere in the bowels of the house. She had lived in apartments all her life; it was going to be a challenge owning a home and shouldering all the responsibilities that came with it.

She paced contemplatively down the full length of the empty living room, her sneakers making no sound on the wooden floor and rug. She sipped her wine as she walked, looking proudly around her. The ceilings were incredibly high, making the house seem larger than it was. Two pairs of French doors – one on either side the room – led out onto the front porch. She would need to buy some comfortable patio furniture. Spring would be here soon and the porch would be a wonderful place to read and write and drink wine while watching the sun set between the trees. She pitied Steve, still stuck in their old apartment, but he hadn't wanted to leave, and he hadn't inherited a house in the country either.

Smiling smugly, she returned to the kitchen for some cheese. She cut herself a sinfully big chunk of creamy Havarti, topped off her wine glass, and headed for the small room where she already knew she would spend most of her time. Tomorrow – after she had weathered the storm of the movers – she would set up her computer and examine the books Robert had left her. She had brought a small lamp and a pack of light bulbs, and she toyed with the idea of plugging it in so she could light a fire, but she was tired and it seemed like too much work. *I'll just wait until tomorrow night*, she thought, and happily added this pleasure to her growing To Do list. It was important that she line up lots of little things to look forward to – stepping stones helping her cross a torrential river of loss as she didn't dare wonder yet what awaited her on the other side. It would be intensely cozy to light a fire her first night alone, but she didn't have the energy to open the flue and make absolutely sure the chimney wasn't clogged so she didn't foolishly risk burning the house down.

For an instant Sofia was overwhelmed by all the responsibilities suddenly placed in her inexperienced hands, but a hearty swallow of Chardonnay helped her feel relaxed and positive again. Challenges were good, they exercised her brain and kept her body occupied. Besides, she trusted Robert not to have left her any major problems to deal with. Next she flirted with the idea of relaxing in a hot bath, but filling the tub and unpacking towels and soap also felt like too much work.

She returned to the kitchen, very pleased with the black counters and glass-fronted cabinets in which she could display all the different colorful dishes and glasses she had collected. A narrow wooden door led into a small utility and storage room equipped with a washer and dryer that, like the refrigerator, were brand-new. The operating manuals and warranties for all three appliances sat on top of the dryer in their respective plastic bags, along with the receipt from *Conn's*. Robert must have left instructions in his Will that they be bought and installed immediately upon his death. His generosity and forethought made her feel miserable again, but she had exhausted herself crying; all she had the energy to do now was make herself a ham and cheese sandwich. She took it out into the living room along with another glass of wine, this one a Merlot, and sat cross-legged in the middle of the rug devouring her meager dinner. She had left the porch light on, and the silhouettes of bare trees surrounding her on three sides were slightly sinister yet also companionable simply because they were life forms more similar to hers in form than all the other species invisibly populating the cold winter night. Then, abruptly, the steady electric glow annoyed her. Determinedly chewing on her last bite of bread, she got up and impulsively turned off all the lights, inside and out.

For a few seconds she couldn't see anything, then the subtle glow of moonlight filtered into her pupils. The night wasn't completely black; the half moon was casting more than enough light to navigate by.

Cradling her wine glass in both hands like a sacred chalice, Sofia walked through the dark house into her new bedroom. The massive bed looked almost frightening by moonlight. After she finished crying she had discovered there were clean, cotton sheets covering a divinely soft feather mattress. She would sleep and dream in luxurious comfort tonight mysteriously cradled by Robert's generous spirit. Sleeping Beauty's bed waiting for her gave her the energy to stay awake and explore because part of her had been asleep for far too long while she was living with Steve, wanting so much to love and be loved. Robert had freed her by taking over the responsibility of giving her the affection and security she needed without demanding anything from her, except that she wake up completely to who she was without being afraid anymore.

One side of the room was dominated by the bed, the other by yet another pair of French doors, and she was thrilled to find a second porch opening up off the bedroom. It wasn't attached to the front porch; it was its own separate little platform into the woods. She unlocked the door, and then closed it behind her to keep the heat inside as she stepped into the night.

The stars looked even more fervently lovely now that she'd drunk some wine. All her life she had lived with the noise of distant (and not so distant) traffic. She stood listening for this steady technological hum, but all she heard was the subliminal moaning of the wind, barely audible behind the soft rustling of leaves. Yet once she became aware of it she could clearly distinguish this haunting sound that was like deep, dark water flowing beneath the rippling brightness of crickets singing, a vibrant yet soothing music that made her feel unaccountably happy; the high-pitched scraping of hundreds of insect wings somehow leaving the profound silence intact.

She stood looking around her in awe at the soft, diffused black of tree trunks stretching for as far as she could see, the whole world visibly washed in moonlight. She could really understand now how in centuries past people waited every month for the moon to come back—the brightest light their desires had the power to turn on even though it was beyond their control. She could almost literally feel it in her bones how in previous lives she had worshiped the moon, whereas in Baton Rouge she had had to make a concerted effort just to see it. Streetlights, buildings, light pollution, everything had separated her from the earth's one and only satellite. She had been mostly aware of it her during her period, when there was no doubt in her mind the moon pulled on her blood at night. It was part of her PMS seeming to feel the crescent moon scraping her womb and making her period come every month.

Sofia stood with her wine glass forgotten in her hand soaking up the delicate sounds weaving themselves into the underlying velvety stillness, absorbing how absolutely alone she was and strangely loving it. There was literally not another soul for miles. She owned twenty acres of land, twenty mostly forested acres with two open areas. She had seen the clearings on the aerial map the attorney showed her, casually suggesting she might like to put a big vegetable garden in one and a pool or guest house in the other. The back of her property – the direction she was facing now – was the narrowest, and she idly wondered who the land beside hers belonged to. She would have to meet her neighbors eventually, far away as they were. A woman living alone needed friends, people she could call in case of an emergency, but she didn't pursue this train of thought as it only made her anxious and she was determined to be optimistic about the future.

It was early, not even eight o'clock, but she was so exhausted by the last tumultuous week she was ready to go to bed and sleep for another seven days. She was turning to go back inside when she glimpsed a flicker of light out in the open field beyond her trees. The red spark swiftly grew larger as she watched. Something had caught fire. She glanced anxiously back into the house. She had brought a cordless phone with her, but she hadn't plugged it in yet. The attorney had assured her all the utilities had been turned on, and she wondered if she should dial 911 and have them call the fire department. She looked back out across the field. The fire was burning strongly and steadily now, yet it seemed contained, and she laughed inwardly at herself for being such an ignorant city slicker. Someone had lit a bonfire, that was all, they were probably burning their trash, or whatever.

Now that she was no longer worried about the conflagration, Sofia found herself staring at it gratefully. It seemed a symbol of something... of her heart rising from the ashes of her old life. Whoever her neighbor was, he had given her a sign she deeply appreciated. She sensed (and it pleased her to imagine) that the person she couldn't see out there was a *he*.

She stood outside a while longer watching the distant fire, until the cold began getting to her and she turned to go back inside. Her body was stiff, but there was a soft smile on her lips.

Chapter Three

Sofia lay in bed reading by the soft light of the lamp she had brought with her. She was propped up against the luxuriously oversized feather pillows feeling she had found her own little corner of heaven. Once she slipped beneath the sheets she discovered that she was physically exhausted but not sleepy, so she reached down into her briefcase, which she had placed next to the bed, and pulled out the book she was writing a paper on.* She had only been in the country a few hours, yet already the centuries' old poems resonated inside her much more intimately and significantly than they had in the city. She opened the dark-green hardback at random, and read quietly out loud to the attentively silent house around her:

SONG*

Two birds flew into the sunset glow
And one of them was my love, I know.
Ah, had it but flown to my heart, its nest!
Two maidens down to the harvest go,
And one of them is my own, I know.
Ah, had she but come to me here, it were best!
Two stars remembered the long ago—
And one of them was my heart's great woe.
If it had but forgotten, and paled in the west!

She rested the book against her chest and gazed up at the dark ceiling. She saw again the silhouettes of cows grazing against the dying light as she drove down the lonely road, contrasted by Magnolia leaves gleaming intimately in her headlights, and the encouraging crowd of stars that greeted her when she stepped out of the car.

"I'm going to love living out here," she whispered, scornfully ignoring the part of her that was frightened and homesick for the city's illusion of companionship, where other people often lived right behind your walls and beneath your feet. She knew she was much safer alone out here in the middle of nowhere, yet she had made the rounds of the house twice before she got into bed to be absolutely sure all the doors were locked. She had also left the porch light on, mainly for her own reassurance; its illumination would only make it easier for anyone trying to break in, a stupid thought she angrily suppressed. Maybe if the windows and the French doors had come with curtains she would feel less vulnerable and exposed, but she would just have to get over her irrational paranoia because fabric would only ruin the view, and made no sense whatsoever in a place where her nearest neighbor lived miles away. She would simply have to drag her childish feelings along behind her more mature reason. Curtains weren't necessary, there was no one looking in on her where she lay in bed wearing only a skimpy white T-shirt. She had always hated sleeping with anything much on, and she wasn't about to begin now.

She lifted the book, randomly opened it up to another page, and began reading softly out loud again...

STILLBORN*

Amid the sprouting seeds flowers, too, are growing,
And so they drink the rain
That the sky sends upon the sprouting seeds.
The threshold of thy cottage is so wet
Because last night such heavy dew hath fallen.

Woman! take up thy life once more
Where thou hast left it,
Nothing is changed for thee, thou art the same,

Thou, who didst think
That all things would be wholly changed for thee.
No dirge doth echo through the dwelling-place,
One cannot mourn as dead
That which hath never lived.

Well, that certainly was relevant to her situation. Her wonderful relationship with Steve never really existed objectively, only in her stubborn imagination. The poem was clearly about a stillborn child, but she had similarly nurtured the idea of being with her one true love and soul mate for seven years in the womb of her soul; she could relate to the sentiment.

Yet had I made for him a dirge so sweet!
Telling therein, that he was all thy hope,
And that he did not well
To go ere he had looked upon the world—
To think so ill of what he ne'er had seen.
Woman! while thou didst bear him, hast thou ever
Told him of graves? or spoken of the sorrow
Of barren wombs?
Didst thou not tell him of thy womb's rejoicing
Over his life?
And that spring sometimes comes upon this earth,
And that some souls there are, that do remember?

Nay, thou didst think on sorrow
While thou hadst joy within thee;
And sorrow frightened him.
Thou didst not tell him, that thy cottage-windows
Looked toward the plain;
That rivers love the flowers upon their banks,
And that the storks come home;
That there are birds that sing, and men as well,
And that their songs are sweet.
Nay, but thou spak'st to him of graves, and so
Their rest grew dear to him.
Now can I make no tender dirge o'er him;
I never saw him live.
Return thee to thy hearth,
And think of him before thine empty hearth;
Saying, while thou dost muse of him:
"How empty is my hearth!"
Toward thy husband stretch thou forth thy hand
With gentle smile, that he
May smile again, and think of Death no more.
For Death it was not
That passed through this thy house—but it was Life
That would not take up her abode therein.
Thou didst but ask him from afar:
"Wilt thou indeed be mine?"—

As one may ask the stars,
The stars reply: "Nay, we belong to no one."
Thou didst but say to him from afar:
"I love thee!"
Even as one may say it to the sky;
The sky makes answer: "Nay, the love of men
Is nought to me!"
Go, woman, to thy daily work again—
Nothing is changed for thee.

Amid the sprouting seeds flowers, too, are growing,
And so they drink the rain
That the sky sends upon the sprouting seeds.
The threshold of thy cottage is so wet
Because last night such heavy dew hath fallen.

* * *

She woke up and thought wildly, *Who turned on the outside lights?!* It was her fourth night in the house, and she had forced herself to become brave enough to sleep in the dark, yet the back porch was lit up by a bright white light that had cut into her psyche and roused her from a dream she sensed she hadn't wanted to leave even though she couldn't recall any details. It took her a few sleepy seconds to understand the full moon was staring down at her house and land. The illumination was so intense, impenetrable shadows were outlined with the sharpness of a sword's edge. She propped herself up against the pillows and lay gazing out through the French doors, glad of the silently demanding company. If the moon had the power to swell ocean tides, it certainly wasn't far-fetched to believe it had the same effect on the blood flowing through her brain, stirring up exceptionally vivid dreams.

She had been so busy since she moved in the days had flown by. She still had much to do – and a lot to buy – but for now she was very pleased with the room in which she spent most of her time. The rest of the house would have to wait. She told herself that everything would fall into place later, gradually, when she had a life again, whatever that meant. She did-n't know anyone in her neighborhood yet. Her mother, and now her best friend, were dead, she had never known her father and her lover was his-tory, she was an only child and she had never been big on casual acquain-tances. She was more alone than ever, yet in a strange way she was enjoy-ing her own company.

The moon shone directly through the French doors, forging black bars across her diamond-paned comforter. It was very cold in the house (she kept the heat turned down at night because it helped her sleep more deeply) yet she couldn't resist pushing the sheets and comforter off her to expose the thin white T-shirt clinging to her torso. She peeled it off impulsively, and the vision of her breasts bouncing into freedom inspired her to kick the blankets away completely. She was only thirty-three-years-old, still quite young, she reminded herself, and she hadn't felt naked like this in a long time. Essentially (if not literally) Steve had always been on top of her; she hadn't experienced her flesh with such intimate, urgent clarity in years.

Suddenly, Sofia felt passionately in love with her body. She began caressing herself with both hands, marveling at the silky smoothness and warmth of her skin. She was beautiful, she could have any man she wanted...

This trite (and not necessarily true) thought comforted her yet also depressed her, and she pushed it away impatiently. She didn't want to think about dating and all the effort she would have to make to get to know complete strangers again, forced into mouthing polite conversation in the unlikely hope she would be inspired to share her deepest thoughts and feelings with them in the future. She didn't want a man to take her out to dinner, she wanted him to fuck her, *really* fuck her. He wouldn't just coolly bang her the way Steve had, he would somehow penetrate her on all levels of her being. He would fuck her like she had never been fucked before, no hesitant tenderness or political correctness holding him back...

The bars of shadow cast by the moon across her bed were so black they almost looked substantial. She gazed down in growing arousal at where the darkness intersected with her thighs, her pale skin absorbing the moonlight. It was almost as though she was being put in a haunting form of bondage...

She reached behind her and pulled a pillow below her head as she pushed herself down the bed, deliberately placing herself directly beneath the checkerboard pattern of light and dark. Her heartbeats quickened as her excitement mysteriously deepened... her beautiful and vulnerable naked body was lying across an altar adorned with ritual black stripes slicing across her breasts, belly and thighs. Insubstantial as they were, the shadows exerted a evocative pressure against her flesh as she willingly laid beneath them. Her body was remembering the dream that eluded her because her pussy was warm and wet, waiting for the man who wasn't there and yet was... she scarcely needed to exercise her imagination to see his face above her sculpted by moonlight and darkness... the face of the man who had painted the black lines across her naked body as part of a dark rite they were both willingly a part of... She had seen this man before, in the daydreams she desperately indulged in the last few times Steve made love to her – a fiercely handsome man with features shaped by other centuries, yet his penetrating stare was hard, totally present, and she distinctly made out his timeless goatee—black as the shadows cast by the full moon— around his firm, determined mouth, and even though she knew he could easily smile, he wasn't doing so now...

Her clitoris felt energized by the full moon over her house as she pressed three fingertips against it, losing herself in a waking dream, her eyes focused on the empty space just above her in which the energy of her imagination merged with invisible forces to create the man she desired more than anything. He wasn't smiling because he was too intent on fucking her, one of his strong hands pinning both her wrists above her head as he penetrated her, his other hand clutching her throat. He didn't comfortably bury himself inside her; he pulled all the way out of her body and forced the full experience of his erection on her pussy over and over again, stroking her hard and deep. His eyes never left hers; she saw that he was completely aware of what he was doing as his grip tightened on her throat and aroused her more than any man ever had. Her intense excitement rose from the mysterious core of her being – from the dark depths of her soul in which her clitoris glowed like the moon, her body absolutely submissive beneath his as he put all his strength into possessing her. Even her sex was powerless to cling to him as his cock stabbed her more swiftly and violently, her legs seeming to levitate around him as she willingly opened herself up to his thrusts, as if there was truly no limit to how far he could drive himself inside her. He was cutting off her breath, and with a small, insignificant part of her mind she was amazed by how real the fantasy was. It didn't feel like her own hand wrapped around her throat, and the man's face was so distinct her body didn't doubt for an instant he was really there with her. The impenetrable darkness of the night allied with the moonlight was using her own limbs to work a powerful magic on her. In the end it didn't matter at all that she was the one bringing herself to a climax with her fingertips as she stopped breathing altogether for a few divinely taut seconds. She climaxed so fiercely she couldn't make a sound as she was overcome by the terribly transcendent certainty that there were other men waiting to take her like this... that he was only the first, and always the last...

Sofia lay across her dream bed as though she had just fallen from a great height, her heart pounding. There was no question about it, she had just had one of the most intense orgasms of her life. It's a scientific fact that almost all parts of a woman's brain are active during sex. There might not have been a cock inside her, but her every mental and physical synapse had been involved in the experience. Only when her pulse slowed down to a more sedate pace did she feel a little disturbed by the morbid nature of the visualization that had turned her on so much. She had read enough to know that most women indulged in dark fantasies; they were common aphrodisiacs even for the most theoretically sedate housewife. However, autoerotic asphyxiation was definitely one of the more dangerous kinks, and she felt vaguely ashamed about filling the room meant for an innocent little girl with such violent images and feelings. But that was ridiculous since this was her bedroom now and, she had to admit, she was seriously enjoying the erotic vibes she was discovering in it. The moon was slowly moving away as the earth turned, only the very foot of the bed still glowed with its attention, yet still she lay naked above the sheets reluctant to let go of her dream man.

It wasn't until she began getting cold that she got out of bed, intending to use the bathroom, but a shaft of moonlight pulled her over to the French doors like a cosmic leash. Her forest was positively flooded with light. The outline of every single branch was so sharp that a few yards away between the trees she distinctly saw a shadow move. She stepped quickly away from the door and pressed herself back against the wall even as she told herself not to jump to conclusions, that the shadow could have been anything, a deer, a young tree swaying in the breeze, *anything*.

She walked quickly into the bathroom and closed the door, turning on the overhead light, bathing herself in normalcy. She sat on the toilet for much longer than necessary, psychoanalyzing her reactions. Obviously, she was feeling guilty about her intensely masochistic fantasy and punishing herself with the much more rational delusion of an intruder wandering her property. She was pathetic. This was the sort of profoundly wishy-washy behavior that had kept her trapped in the wrong relationship for so long, and if she wasn't careful, she would continue making the same vital mistakes over and over again no matter who she ended up dating.

By the time she wiped herself clean and flushed, she had decided it would be wrong (not to mention impossible) to censor her fantasies. If she imagined a man cutting off her breath while he fucked her, then so be it, there had to be a reason for it, and she couldn't deny something that aroused her so much whether she ever really experienced it or not.

She slipped back into bed mentally chanting, *There's no one outside! There's no one outside!* She shivered as she pulled the sheets and the heavy feather comforter up to her chin. It was three-thirty-three in the morning, and she had lost all the delicious body heat she had accumulated sleeping. She wished there was a fireplace in the bedroom. Now *that* would be cozy, if dangerous.

The moon remained demandingly bright, and she couldn't get back to sleep no matter how hard she tried, so she switched on the bedside light and opened *The Bard of the Dimbovitza* to a random page again…

In the Moonlight*

Tomorrow,
The days of gladness will be done for me;
Heavy and overcast my soul will be,
And day will seem like night for me to-morrow.

Maria Isabel Pita

His spade he cast aside,

And told us all the story of his grief.

And thus he spake to us: "I had a daughter,

Gay silver spangles she was wont to wear.

"Father," she said,

"Which is the way that leadeth to the plain?

I love the plain, when the moon looks thereon,

And I would have the moon look, too, on me."

I followed her, one evening,

My child I followed down into the plain,

And then I saw how the moon looked on her,

While she held converse with a dead man there.

She gently stroked his head, and gave him drink,

And showed him all the loveliness of earth.

Between them stood the cross from off his grave.

I heard the dead man ask her:

"What dost thou all day long upon the earth?"

My child made answer: "I await the night."

Then he went hence, bearing his cross away,

And hence my daughter went, bearing her grief,

Then dead upon the earth I stretched my child,

That so she might be one with him, the dead,

Yea, then I slew my child.

Tomorrow,

The days of gladness will be done for me;
Heavy and overcast my soul will be,
And day will seem like night for me to-morrow.

Sofia quickly set the book back down on the nightstand, but she didn't turn off the light.

Chapter Four

The sun glimmering between the trees lured her outside after she finished her toast and tea sitting in the big green chair by the cold fireplace. Last night's violent climax and shadowy fears seemed more unreal than the dreams she couldn't remember.

It was a gorgeous day again. The sky above the trees was a deep and brilliant blue that very soon would be dabbed with the luminous light-green paint flecks of budding leaves. Spring would be here in a few weeks, and on such stunningly clear days the temperature was an ideal sixty-five degrees in the sunlight, a touch cooler in the shade, or if a wind was blowing in from the southeast across her neighbor's field.

Sofia followed one of the paths leading away from the house, amazed she didn't have to drive anywhere to take a walk through the woods. She explored a little every day unless it was raining. Hurricanes Katrina and Rita didn't appear to have done much damage here. She had come across a handful of fallen trees, but for all she knew they might have been that way for years and not been downed by the storms at all. It thrilled her that she had yet to reach all the borders of her property, which the aerial map had shown was completely fenced in.

She slipped her hands into the pockets of her lavender fleece jacket as she walked beneath the trees, enjoying the way the cool breeze played with her long, golden-brown hair. Birds were calling urgently to each other all around her. She could distinguish at least two songs, one especially lovely, plaintive melody contrasted by another shriller, less complex series of notes. She knew nothing about birds, and more than once she was amazed to look up and discover the most powerful music emanating from the tiniest breast. A bird's throat was an enchanted instrument, indeed, that made her wish she had a lovely singing voice like Princess Aurora so she could contribute to the woodland chorus. She was surprised some crickets were still vibrating in broad daylight, their energetic chirping reminding her that everything around her was actually just a bunch of sub-atomic particles assuming the form of a forest and of a lovely woman walking through it. Everything was energy that only appeared solid thanks to the haunting artist of the human brain commanding the universe like its own personal Monet, and the truly interesting thing was that she had the power to think about the interpretive magic her brain was so casually performing every second.

She missed talking to Robert about her metaphysical thoughts and everything else. Until he was gone she hadn't realized what a wonderful verbal shorthand they had developed between them over the years. She missed him so much it literally hurt when, at least once or twice a day, she was forced to stop whatever she was doing when she began crying and couldn't stop. She didn't miss Steve at all. In fact, with every second that passed, her relief at being free from him only deepened.

A swift rustling across the crisp carpet of dead leaves made her pause and watch two grey squirrels running up a tree. They performed death-defying acrobatics leaping between the flimsiest top-most branches with a reckless speed that made her breath catch as she tried to imagine herself doing that. She smiled wondering what they were up to. Did they store their nuts up so high or were they simply having fun? It was impossible to tell, and she didn't really care, she was just happy they were there.

She continued walking wondering how long she could endure such bucolic peace without going crazy. She searched inside herself for an honest answer, and was happy to discover that the reply was a fervent *forever*. She didn't miss BR anymore than she did Steve. In only a few days her exboyfriend and the city had become synonymous in her psyche, and she was nothing but glad to be free of them and on her own. She would have to go back to teaching eventually, but there was no earthly reason to think about that now; a year from now felt a lifetime away and so much (she hoped) could happen between now and then.

Sofia concluded she must have done something right to suddenly find herself in such a beautiful place. Native Americans understood you can never own the land, and it was true. With every passing day the line between her feelings and the sensuality of her property became more and more blurred, until she suspected that one day it would hardly exist at all.

When she reached one of the two large open areas, she stood warming herself beneath the sun. Later in the day the temperature would start dropping and she would have the pleasure of lighting a fire again. A burning log was the best company of all sometimes, the crackling of wood being consumed as eloquent as the most profound conversation. Sitting on an oversized pillow warmed by the gray hearthstones, she felt wonderfully close to Robert in the evenings. As she sipped her Chardonnay gazing out the window watching the sun set between the trees in the west, she would talk to him in her head and be sure he heard her somehow, the silence of the house he had left her a profound response that mysteriously answered all her questions by reminding her of how much she had to do. She had to make this her home. She had to plant the seeds of a new life here and believe in the harvest of future happiness and fulfillment.

How she was ever going to meet people (especially so-called eligible men) out "in the middle of nowhere" was the really important question. She had to believe in Fate. If she was destined to meet her soul mate, it didn't matter where she lived. Yet could she really believe that? Firstly, *was* there such a thing as a soul mate? In the beginning she had thought Steve was the one, hadn't she? She had been wrong, but that hardly disproved the theory of true love. She could only hope. Hope was everything, and Robert's last letter helped to stoke it passionately inside her whenever she read it again for reassurance and company. But secondly, even if she did continue believing in a man she was meant to be with, how *was* she going to meet him? Reality wasn't a Disney cartoon, he wasn't going to ride his valiant steed through the forest one afternoon and spy her between the trees singing along with the birdies.

She turned back towards the house, once more deliberately not defining the borders of her land, enjoying the intrigue of not knowing exactly where it ended and someone else's property began. She was also itching to get online. Bless Robert for understanding she could not possibly live without the internet. Probably on the same day her refrigerator and washer and dryer were delivered a Satellite dish was installed on her roof, and last night, after dinner, she hadn't been able to resist creating a profile on match.com. She used a fake name and a new hotmail account in order not to compromise her LSU e-mail address. She had to do whatever was necessary to take charge of her destiny by making sure Fate had plenty of raw material to work with. The world-wide web made physical distances irrelevant. For all she knew she might end up falling in love with someone who lived in Madagascar. She doubted it, but she was determined to believe anything was possible because it was exciting to be positive and very boring to be cynical.

She followed a different path back to the house which took her out to the mailbox. She had met her postal carrier yesterday as she drove up in a cute little red jeep with flashing lights on top. She was a blonde lady named Kelly who cheerfully informed her that she also delivered stamps, weighed packages and picked up mail, all Sofia had to do was leave it in her box.

The shadow of a hawk glided across the gravel drive, its open wings dark-gold against the lapis-lazuli sky. Her mailbox was empty, but that was okay, it was too early for Kelly to have made her rounds yet, and it gave her an excuse to walk out here again later that afternoon.

She thought about how nice it would be to have a dog or a cat or both as she followed the winding driveway back home. The apartment she had lived in with Steve had allowed small pets, but for some reason they never indulged in one. Yes, she would definitely get herself a nice big dog, for protection as well as company, and a kitten or two to cuddle with in the evenings. Veterinarian bills were expensive, but she could handle it.

She skipped lightly up the porch steps, cheered by the prospect of a devoted canine companion and a sensual pair of felines even as she wondered how many men had already responded to her ad. That's what it was really, she was "selling" herself and all her charms to potential suitors/buyers, yet she hated thinking about it that way. In her mind she was simply giving Fate material to work with, and a possible stage to play itself out on.

A large wicker basket was sitting in front of her door. She stared down at it, not quite able to comprehend the sight, and she avoided making sense of it for a minute by watching a red squirrel climb head-first out of a Tulip tree, busily talking to itself. It was much bigger and fluffier than a gray squirrel, with a white face like a mask, and as it disappeared beneath her car, she looked back down at the basket. She crouched beside it and inspected its contents with a curious wonder. It was filled with food, but there was no brand name on anything; it all appeared to be home-made. The basket contained a small circle of semi-soft white cheese in plastic wrap; an old-fashioned looking half-pint milk bottle; a violet nylon net filled with six large, light-brown eggs; a luxurious head of curly spinach; and a gallon-sized plastic bag filled with big shelled pecans.

"Oh, my..." She handled each offering reverently. Someone must have dropped by to welcome her to the neighborhood. "This is so nice!" City dweller that she was, the last thing she had expected was a house-warming present from a complete stranger, but she was living in the country now and things were obviously different out here. She was sorry she had missed whoever had been so thoughtful. She couldn't even see her neighbors' houses, but she had a feeling she was going to get to know them better than she had ever known the people who lived right next door to her in the city.

She carried her gifts into the house and promptly refrigerated them. The eggs had probably come from local hens, the milk from someone's cow or goat along with the cheese, and the Spinach and Pecans were also almost certainly home-grown. She would have to drive well over an hour to get to *Whole Foods* in Baton Rouge. This basket was what organic eating and sustainable farming were all about. The thought occurred to her then that she could do it too, if she wanted to. The fact that she didn't know the first thing about vegetable gardening or raising livestock didn't matter. She was a smart woman, she could learn. It would help keep her busy, and exercise her creativity in a very different way than writing essays on poetry. The Romanian

Lute Player songs she was composing a paper on were all about how the land and the human soul were inseparable from each other. Hard, creative work was what she needed, in every sense, but right now she was dying to check her new hotmail account to see if she'd received any e-mails from sexy men.

* * *

"Ugh, ugh, ugh!" Was the only way to express how she felt about the first responses to her online profile. Incredibly, there were over fifty messages in her Inbox, most of which she immediately deleted for a variety of reasons. A man who had not yet mastered the art of spelling could never be her soul mate. In the end she was left with three candidates, but only one of them had bothered to attach a photograph of himself. Provided that was actually him in the picture (and that it was him in the present, not twenty years ago) he was rather attractive. He was wearing a white dress shirt with the sleeves rolled up to the elbows, and a tantalizing slice of his chest was exposed beneath his broad shoulders. His legs looked strong if a little squat in tight blue jeans, but she blamed that on the camera angle. His blonde hair appeared to be thinning a little, but for the moment it was all still there, and the laugh lines at the corners of his eyes and of his smiling mouth were appealing. He was too far away for her to make out the color his eyes, but according to his profile they were blue, and he was clean shaven. He had been a professor of Economics at Tulane University in New Orleans before Hurricane Katrina, but the severe faculty cuts had forced him to relocate to Baton Rouge, where he was fortunate (well connected) enough to be welcomed into the LSU fold. There was nothing wrong with him that she could see, certainly nothing to prevent her from writing him back thanking him for getting in touch. She didn't commit herself to anything or attach another photo of herself. The two pictures she had put up on her profile had been hard enough to come by as it was. She owned dozens of CD's full of digital images, but Steve had taken most of the recent photos she had of herself, and maybe that was why she never looked as good in them as she thought she did in reality, a forced smile being worse than no smile at all. So she posted two images of her captured by Robert late one afternoon beneath one of the magnificent old oak trees growing on campus. The first one was a full body shot of her in a sleeveless violet dress she had worn to some reception or other, her cleavage, slender figure and long legs accentuated by the tight bodice and the diaphanous skirt beneath it blowing in the wind. She was wearing white high-heeled sandals and holding a small white while with her other hand she laughingly kept the hair our out of her eyes. The second one was a close-up of her face taken the same day. Her light-brown eyes were averted in a way that made her soft smile look sad in a wondering sort of way... as though she was seeing the future when Robert would be dead and Steve history and she was living alone posting this image of herself online in the hope of catching her true love...

If the professor asked her out she might agree to meet him for lunch at *Louis*. After all, she had to make a trip into BR soon to go to *Whole Foods*, and that way she could be home well before nightfall and avoid driving down lonely country roads in the dark.

Chapter Five

It was overcast and dark all the next day, and the dramatic change in the weather completely demoralized her. All the mental and emotional steps she had taken not to become depressed vanished with the sunlight and she was left at square one – a gravestone marking the death of all the love in her life. She chided herself for being so dependent on the sun's cosmic vitamin D, but to no avail. She turned on all the lights and lamps she possessed in an effort to dispel the gloom, but she did absolutely nothing except wait for nightfall when she could at least drink some wine and light a fire. She listened to NPR for a while, but news of war, disease, famine and overall government corruption throughout the world did nothing to improve her mood. She was forced to turn the radio off and listen to the silence.

Sofia had never experienced such silence. The whole world was subdued; not even birds were singing the day was so dreary. The only thing that relieved the oppressive gloom was a vigorous wind blowing in from the southeast. She couldn't remember wind like this in Baton Rouge and at LSU where she was always surrounded by buildings. There was a front moving in and she kept waiting for it to begin thundering and raining, but even though a gentle drizzle darkened the tree trunks, no tumultuous atmospheric relief was forthcoming. It didn't rain, it didn't storm – the day just never chose to dawn, that was all – and by the time six o'clock and Chardonnay time rolled around, she could not have felt more miserably lethargic.

She had gone for a walk at around three clock, defying the sky to open up when she was farthest from the house, gambling with the elements. She followed the gravel road all the way to the edge of her property from where she could see rolling meadows and horses peacefully grazing. She stood gazing out at them for a while because she had nothing better to do, and because they were beautiful. Her favorite was a chocolate-brown horse, his flowing blonde mane a sensually striking contrast to his sleek, dark flanks. She knew no more about horses than she did about birds – her ignorance of animal life was truly appalling – but she knew beauty when she saw it, and for a long while she couldn't take her eyes off the muscular bodies that were using only a slight fraction of their power to walk contentedly across the nourishing grass. It was humbling how sedately unaware they remained of her tormented humanity. Her brain felt like a roiling grey cloud trapped in the firmament of her skull. The horses bore the oppressive weight of the drop in air pressure easily, the earth's atmosphere a mysterious saddle over their ancient backs. After a while she couldn't stand their indifference any longer and headed back. Her challenge had not been met – it didn't rain, it didn't thunder, it was simply depressingly dark all afternoon, and the wind kept blowing as though on its way somewhere more exciting, leaving Clinton suspended and longing for a sensual release that never came.

Her second day in the house she had driven into Zachary for groceries, but she still wasn't eating the tasty, balanced diet she was accustomed to. Tonight she was very grateful for the fresh head of curly spinach and the moist, crumbly white cheese she used to make herself a salad, tossing in some whole pitted black olives. The pecans also served as a delicious and nutritious snack to have with her white wine, and as an entrée to go with her salad she fried up two of the fresh eggs and served them over-easy over some brown rice. A glass of red wine to accompany the rustic feast, and she found herself happier than she had been in over twelve hours eating across from a crackling fire. Nevertheless, it was a relief when it was late enough to go to sleep. She prayed it would be sunny again tomorrow. The LSU professor had not yet written back after she responded to his e-mail, and she was at once relieved and disappointed as she slipped beneath the sheets. Already she had a backlog of new e-mails she hadn't gone through yet. She needed all the positive energy she could muster to deal with so many disappointing (and often disgusting) suitors.

The moon and the stars were only a memory. There was a layer of clouds concealing the sky, and that restless wind was still blowing. A tree branch tapped against a window just as she was sinking into sleep, making her open her eyes and stare alertly into the darkness... it was as if someone wanted to get in and was communicating with her by way of a haunting Morse Code...

Sofia has no idea how long she managed to sleep before something else woke her. The wind had finally dropped, she could tell that right off because the house was cold and silent as a mausoleum around her. It was so cold, in fact, that she had decided to wear a long white nightgown to bed. She got up, drawn like a moth to the light glimmering far away between the trees out in the field bordering her property. She wondered at the sight, for the middle of the night was hardly the time to casually light a bonfire, yet she was glad of the vivid red flames as she felt their heat even through the window panes. The fire was large and vigorous. She had missed the sun desperately, and now a piece of it had fallen to earth to comfort her, burning like a star. She couldn't resist opening the French doors and stepping out onto her porch. She was surprised to discover that it was much chillier in her bedroom than it was out in nature. It didn't matter that she was barefoot and sleeveless; it felt absolutely right to step off the smooth wooden boards onto the cool and prickly grass softened by a welcoming carpet of dead leaves. The fire was so animated, so beautiful, all she wanted was to be closer to it. At first she walked slowly, tentatively, not quite sure what she was doing, but then all at once she began running towards the blaze as though her life depended on it; her heart pounding in rhythm with the flames fervently licking the wood sustaining them. The aerial photo of her land had indicated there was a fence surrounding her acreage, but nothing got in her way as she lifted her nightgown up to her knees to keep from tripping on it.

She stopped a few feet away from the bonfire, her chest rising and falling from how quickly and eagerly she had run towards it. One of the thin straps of her gown slipped off her shoulder, but she didn't notice, enraptured by the conflagration, her chilled skin experiencing the roaring heat as a profoundly relaxing warmth. The wall of fire was wider than her bed and as tall as the man who stepped around from behind it. She let the white cotton drift softly around her ankles again, the slackening of her fingers the only physical reaction she was capable of as he effortlessly ripped open her nightgown. He was wearing heavy black gloves, the sort of gloves used by Medieval noblemen when they went hunting with their falcons – thick black leather gloves that protected his wrist when the bird of prey's claws clung to it obediently, descending from the freedom of the open sky onto its master's arm. He tore her nightgown open all the way down in front as easily as paper, and then flung the useless cloth – *white as a shroud*, she thought – into the flames. The features of his face forged by firelight and shadow were those of a stranger and yet somehow utterly familiar. His expression was inscrutably hard, like the hilt of a sword she also recognized; her deepest feelings immediately grasping how desperately she wanted him as desire sliced right through her fear. His body was an inescapable silhouette seducing her with the heady scent of sleek leather, rough and smooth, earthy and polished all in one breath as he cupped her breasts and began viciously sucking on her nipples, moving ravenously from one to the other. She clung to his gloved wrists, weakened by an intense longing to submit to him absolutely no matter what he did to her. He growled deep in his throat, and an irresistible pleasure welled up inside her, flowing sweet and hot into his mouth like a divine milk that could never be spilled but only relished forever while the fire hissed as though her juicing pussy was making the hard logs steam...

She was barely conscious of spreading herself back across the grass, not sure if her knees gave way or if he pushed her down or if they fell together. It was an immense relief when she at last felt him determinedly gripping her ankles. He forced her legs together as he lifted them all the way up and back, pinning them down around her face. If it hadn't been for the glimmering red and gold threads in his leather vest she wouldn't have been able to see him at all as his invisible erection swiftly stabbed her. She gasped because his hard-on seemed to sink to the very hilt of her being. She couldn't see his cock but she could distinctly feel it's thick and rigid length opening her up, her innermost flesh shaping itself to the relentlessly demanding dimensions of his lust. The position he held her down in made it impossible for her to defend herself from the breathtaking force of his thrusts. She wanted to cry "Oh, God, yes! Yes!" but she couldn't speak he was fucking her so violently, his cool balls slapping against her hot crack as he drove himself deeper and deeper into her body. He abruptly let go of her ankles and her legs fell open around him as he cruelly clutched both her tender breasts, bracing himself on them. His full weight digging into her chest threatened to cut off her breath but she didn't try to push him away; she remained totally passive beneath him because this was what she wanted more than anything else in the world – to mysteriously offer him her very soul by letting him use her body however he desired.

She was stunned yet somehow not surprised when another man suddenly knelt behind her and caressed the soft warm skin of her neck with his cold gloved hands. At last she made a sound – a small, questioning, yet still utterly submissive moan as he turned her head gently to one side. She kept her eyes open as the man driving his pulsing erection into her body sank his teeth into the side of her throat, his triumphant groan echoed by a rumble of thunder as all the restless shadows cast by the bonfire began taking the form of tall silhouettes separating themselves from the darkness to surround her. Then there was a blinding flash... of excruciating disappointment when, abruptly, she woke up.

* * *

"Oh, thank God!" she said out loud when morning brought sunshine and a clear sky, the deep yet radiant beauty of which could not be described simply by calling it blue. It was impossible to define all the good things the sight of such a sky did to her psyche. Nevertheless, the previous day's pregnant gloom felt worthwhile today because it had given birth to the most vivid erotic dream of her life. She wondered if Robert would approve of her darkly sensual response to the land he had willed her. She had never shared her sexual fantasies with him; it was the only part of her she hadn't revealed to him, and she wondered if he could see inside her now from wherever he was. She almost hoped not. She had never thought of herself as submissive. Steve had always played along with *her* fantasies, and yet they *had* usually involved her being tied up or dominated in some way. Her subconscious was coming clean, letting her know she possessed an intense masochistic streak. Yet her dream was only a fantasy. She suspected the reality would be very different, and she had no desire to be bitten. Maybe once or twice she had imagined being possessed by a sexy vampire, but what red-blooded heterosexual female hadn't? It seemed her relationship with Steve had acted as a damn, and when it broke, desires and inclinations she had suppressed welled up to the surface of her consciousness, and now they were threatening to drown all caution in the haunting depths of her libido. Perhaps this was the price she paid for how long she sipped her fantasies inside a safe – yet ultimately unhealthy and destructive – relationship.

Sofia was both disturbed and aroused by her dream, by how breathtakingly real it had felt, and by how terribly disappointed she had been when it came to an end. She could sense her ordeal had only just begun, that countless men would have fucked her if she hadn't woken up. They would have taken turns with her, they wouldn't have used all three of her orifices at once, that would have come later as part of another, and even more devastating, ritual…

She got of bed in an effort to escape the frustrated longing that gripped her thinking about those last, deliriously promising seconds in the dream as the man possessing her groaned so deep in his throat it sounded like a growl as he ejaculated endlessly inside her, his penis pulsing against the silky walls of her pussy sheathing his stabbing erection so that she clearly felt it mysteriously expanding her deepest, most profoundly submissive being with the force of his fulfillment. He was blessedly beating all the thoughts out of her, transporting her beyond fear as she exulted in the sensation of her blood pulsing into his mouth in rhythm with his thrusts. His teeth and his cock were both unbelievably hard as he opened her up and she juiced helplessly at both ends of her flesh because it felt so unimaginably glorious to be trapped in her body and offering it to him – to all his darkest desires to feed on forever because she never wanted the almost unbearably ecstasy to end. The dangerous power of her excitement was stoked like an all-consuming fire by the violence of his penetrations, until she was so intensely turned on that time and space curved and collapsed into her naked body lying across the grass as she felt herself become the center of everything, the hot and beautiful fount of all life… It wasn't surprising that a fulfillment much deeper and vaster than a climax had short-circuited even her high voltage dream synapses and woken her up.

She walked into the bathroom feeling strangely numb emotionally. After a dream that hot, nothing the day brought could possibly seem interesting. She turned on the tap and gazed at her reflection in the mirror waiting for the water to warm up. Her cheeks were flushed, her eyes were shining, and her tangled hair looked wildly lovely. Very slowly, she reached up and gently extracted a dead golden leaf from where it was ensnared amidst her light-brown strands. She stared at it calmly. It must have been there since yesterday and she hadn't noticed because she was so depressed she didn't even bother to brush her hair before she went to bed.

She tossed the leaf into a little wicker trash can and washed her face. It wasn't until she was applying her daily moisturizing lotion to her cheeks and the skin beneath her chin that she noticed the hickey on her neck. She froze, her reason paralyzed by this impossible evidence of the invisible line between dreams and reality. She draped all her hair over one shoulder and leaned towards the glass to inspect the mark as closely as possible. There were four dark-red dots, two above and two below, roughly three inches apart, and all around them her skin was slightly inflamed down to where her neck flowed into her shoulder blade. She had no idea what a spider bite looked like, but this had to be it. She lived in a forest now; all sorts of creatures could slip between the cracks of her floors and crawl into bed with her. She would have to thoroughly inspect the sheets and mattress tonight before she went to sleep. She dabbed Hydrogen Peroxide on the ugly mark and then slathered it with Neosporin. The last thing she needed was an infection. Obviously, something had bitten her while she was asleep in bed and that's why the man in her dream had turned into a vampire. This explanation made depressing sense. Her reason satisfied, and her feelings so torn between anxiety and longing that she still felt curiously numb, she got on her with her day because there was nothing else she could do.

Chapter Six

The LSU professor wrote her back and said he would be honored to take her out to dinner. She fired off a response saying she would be happy to accept his invitation as long as they could make it lunch. She didn't offer any explanations. She also didn't give him her phone number. She heard back from him almost right away. He would be delighted to take her to lunch today, if she could make it. His unabashed eagerness made her smile. A lot of men would play hard to get or pretend they didn't care when they met. Whatever his faults might turn out to be, Marcus appeared to have his priorities straight, at least. After another set of e-mails, they agreed to meet in *Whole Foods* at noon.

Sofia was thrilled. This was definitely her idea of one-stop shopping. She was so excited to be getting out of the house she giggled like a school girl rushing to get ready for her first date. It had been a long time since she agonized over what to wear. It was chilly out, and this was a very casual meeting, so she chose black yoga pants and a long, form-fitting sage-green cashmere sweater. And over this sexy rustic look, as she thought of it, she slipped on her violet jacket. She left her long hair down, partly to hide the bite on her neck. She thought of putting foundation on it to conceal the sinister looking red puncture marks, but then thought better of it. She had nothing to hide; it wasn't her fault something had bitten her. Marcus might even know what creature it was had come upon her in the middle of the night; he might be able to dispel her dreamy idea of vampires and the much more real concern of infection. She decided to go for the all-natural look and wear hardly any makeup, just a little powder, blush, black eyeliner and a faint touch of lavender lip gloss. She slipped on the pearl drop earrings Robert had given her for her birthday last year, and her delicate gold watch, the only jewelry she deemed appropriate for a casual lunch date in a supermarket.

She made sure all the doors were locked even though she knew perfectly well they were, and let herself out. Now that it was time to go, she found herself reluctant to leave. The sun was shining and the woods looked so beautiful she felt she would be leaving the best parts of herself behind when she drove into the city. Suddenly all she felt like doing was reading in one of the comfortable blue folding chairs she had bought for the porch. But she had a date today; this profoundly simple pleasure would just have to wait until tomorrow. She was surprised and pleased by how hard it was to tear herself away from her new home and the land surrounding it. As she got in the car, she suffered the sobering certainty that this impulsive trip into town was a meaningless distraction and that nothing would come of it except the consolation prize of a kitchen full of delicious food. Yet if going out today served to help her appreciate her newfound contemplative solitude, then so much the better.

It took her over and hour to get to *Whole Foods*. She didn't hurry; driving though the country on a gorgeous day was an invigorating experience. She broke the speed limit only after she reached Baker and ugly little strip malls began dominating the landscape. It was a weekday, but the parking lot of the natural foods store was packed, as usual. No matter how her lunch date turned out, she could still look forward to shopping afterwards, which would be quite an adventure because she was planning to stock up. She had brought her cooler in the trunk, and she would ask for a bag of ice at the meat counter. Now that she lived all the way out on Clinton, she had a good excuse to fill her refrigerator to bursting.

She had agreed to meet Marcus at the Pasta Bar, and she spotted him right away already waiting for her. She watched him for a moment without his knowledge. How could she have forgotten this sinking feeling? She hadn't experienced it in years, but that was no excuse. She should have remembered how depressing it was to agree to go on a date with a man she had never met in the flesh before, and to know the instant she laid eyes on him that he wasn't the one. She had also conveniently forgotten that she was incapable of settling for less – for a sensually stimulating affair and no more, no profound forever, just hot sex served on the tepid platter of friendship. His picture wasn't as recent as she had allowed herself to believe. It was maybe only a year or two old, but a lot could happen to man in that time, especially after a hurricane wiped out his life. He had gained a little weight, and the powerful chest she had admired more than anything else about him in the photograph was swiftly eroding into fat. His shoulders were broad enough to carry it off, but his legs were in fact a bit too short for his torso, and already she could see his bare pink scalp between the comb marks in his fine blonde hair. Superficially speaking, he was still an attractive man, but all she felt looking at him was disappointment, and a slight disgust that she had even entertained the thought of sleeping with him. She made the decision, right then and there, that it was much too soon for her to be looking for love again. She was going to stick to her original plan and spend some quality time with herself alone in the beautiful home Robert had left her so she could do just that.

Not caring now what he thought of her, she approached him confidently, but her intention to write him off tripped uncertainly over his boyish grin. He slipped off the stool and helped her take off her jacket. Surely she knew better than to judge a book by its cover. Maybe she thought she was being deep when in truth she was being completely superficial—a convincing argument presented by her brain that didn't for one second fool the rest of her. He was dressed casually, but his light-blue button-down shirt was still creased in back from the plastic it had come folded and wrapped in. As they talked and ate, everything about him depressed her because it was so familiar and ordinary. She felt trapped in a trite sitcom as her guardian angels watched in appalled silence. The truth was that this pleasant, well educated, handsome man's aura had a mysteriously nauseating effect on her, as if the atmosphere he breathed was different in invisible but vital ways from the one she needed to live despite the fact they were sharing the same physical space.

"Do you shop here often?" he asked, and already she could tell by the obviously teasing quality of his smile that it was a loaded question.

"Now that I live all the way out in Clinton, I only come here once or twice a month to stock up."

"Helping all those small organic farmers stay in business, huh?"

"Yes, why not? Companies like Google and *Whole Foods* give me hope for the future of corporations."

"I agree, basically they're trying to do the right thing," he said complacently, "but the truth is that at least half the produce in this store comes from a handful of big organic farms in California, not from the mom and pop operations they do their best to make us believe it all mostly comes from."

Sofia resented the fact that he was depressing her even more than she already was having lunch with him. She couldn't put her finger on it exactly, but there was something profoundly undefined about him that only became more obvious as he grew older. It was as though the more society molded his every feeling and thought, the more the unique spirit that had taken root in his mother's womb was eroded by life's circumstances to the point where it almost didn't seem to be there anymore. She suspected she was being morosely unfair, but she didn't care. She just wanted this pathetic date to end so she could do some shopping and go home to her trees, and her fireplace, and her dreams...

"And a very high percentage of this beautifully expensive produce," he went on decisively, "comes from South American farms. Personally, I prefer to buy local. A tomato grown in Zachary is much fresher than one grown in Chile."

"No doubt." He was obviously a professor of economics, and even though part of her mind found the conversation interesting, another part of her couldn't stop comparing him to the man in her dream. She knew this was psychologically suspect, but she didn't care about that either. As she picked at her seafood pasta, it became obvious to her that her years with Steve had inoculated her against succumbing to possible mediocre relationships in the future. During those seven years her soul had gotten its PhD on the subject of everything she didn't desire in a lover. She would leave her profile up on match.com, however, in the future she would be *much* more particular about who she met for lunch or dinner.

"I would love to buy local as well," she agreed, "but I really believe in organic, sustainable farming. Whatever its faults, *Whole Foods* is a paragon of virtue compared to most companies."

"That's true, but it's all very complex," he concluded vaguely.

"I'm sure." She finished her bottled water.

"Well," he glanced at his watch abruptly, "I'm afraid I've got to get going. I have another class at two."

"Okay." She didn't know if he was picking up on her negative vibes, or if he simply didn't find her as attractive as her vanity would have liked him to, but it didn't matter. "Thank you for lunch," she added politely. "It was delicious."

"My pleasure." He stood up. "We should do this again sometime soon."

"You know where to reach me." She couldn't help taunting him with the fact that he was leaving empty-handed; all he still had was her e-mail address.

He lightly grasped her arm and gave her a quick peck on the cheek. "Take care," he said, brusquely avoiding her eyes.

She waited until he was out of sight before picking up her napkin and wiping her cheek with it. She wasn't concerned about germs, she just didn't like the cold, wet imprint left by his lips on her skin. Somehow it was worse than the mysterious bite on her neck.

* * *

Sofia got home, put away her groceries, and then hurried out onto the porch to catch the golden rays of the afternoon sun lancing through her forest as it slowly began setting in the west. She brought a cup of hot Chamomile tea outside with her, and she sighed contentedly as she opened *The Bard of the Dimbovitza* and began reading.

SLEEP*

Beneath the poplars by my door
Didst sit thee down,
And on my door didst look, but never enter.
Why dost thou love the poplar's shade so much?

Sleep said: "I know so many things;
Dreams do I know, and sighs.
More than the forest that ceaseless murmurs,
More than the river that weeps, I know,
More than the wind that sings.
And I know more than the hearts of men,
Since I can silence their hearts."
So then the forest, the wind, and the river,
And the hearts of men, all said to Sleep:
"Come, tell us what thou dost know."
Then Sleep replied: "I will tell you softly."–
And he said to them: "Rest I know.
And I know, besides, what the maiden hideth–
What the wife doth not dare to tell,
From the breath of their lips I guess it.
Death envies me, for whoso would find me,
He need not go down to the grave.
And Death speaks thus to me: "Why dost thou let them

Awaken again?" But I let men awaken

That they may hold me more dear.

And I lay a smile on their lips, moreover,

Instead of the tears they have shed,

'Thou hast the face of my heart's beloved,'

The maiden saith to me, and the wife:

'The voice of my husband hast thou.'

Death suffereth me to seek through the graves,

And bring forth those who long have slept

To those who sleep but an hour.

And those who sleep but an hour, they bless me

For giving back those who for long have slept.

'Thou hast the taste of the freshest water,'

The thirsting traveler saith to me.

'Thou hast the look of my home,' saith the wand'rer.

And in his shade the Past doth let me

Seek those who have suffered sore, and bring them

Up before those who made them suffer;

And those who made them suffer, tremble

At sight of those who have suffered sore.

'Lo! thou hast blood upon thy hand!'

Saith the man who hath stained his knife, to me.

'Thou hast a dagger in thy hand,'

Saith the man who hath betrayed, to me.

I am so gentle, yet so dread,

That all mankind is fain to have me,
Because they love me and yet fear.
I dwell in nests, since they are lofty,
In graves, because grass covers them.
And the hearts of men have need of me,
And I have need of their joys and sorrows
To fashion dreams of them.
And he who lies asleep is sacred.
Men say of one who sleeps: 'Heaven loves him;
For see, he sleeps.'
But he who cannot sleep, arouses
Uneasiness in all men's hearts,
They say of him: 'He cannot sleep.'"

Beneath the poplars by my door
Didst sit thee down,
And on my door didst look, but never enter.
Why dost thou love the poplar's shade so much?

It was getting colder, so she set her book down and went inside to make some more hot tea. When she came back outside, a man dressed all in black was sitting in her chair.

"Beautiful." He closed her book and set it down as he stood up, but the intent way his eyes were fixed on her face almost made her wonder what he was referring to.

"Thank you," she replied breathlessly, her heart racing. "I'm writing a paper on it."

He didn't smile as he slipped his hands into the pockets of the black leather jacket he was wearing over black jeans and black boots. "Did I frighten you?" he asked in a deep, quiet voice. He didn't have a southern accent, and his eyes looked almost as black as his goatee.

"Yes... no... a little... it's just that..." She couldn't tell him that he looked impossibly familiar. "I'm Sofia."

"Those poems are quite dark, even violent, yet you love them."

"Yes..." She couldn't take her eyes off his face. "I discovered that book buried in the LSU library. It hadn't been checked out in decades. I was nineteen-years-old and I thought it was so incredible that I read parts of it to all my friends, and suddenly everyone was whispering behind my back that I was a Satan worshipper."

"Are you?"

She laughed.

His eyes held hers. "Did you enjoy your welcome, Sofia?"

"Excuse me?" She remembered her dream and all the men surrounding her naked body hungrily waiting to fuck her and to suck her blood, and God knew what else all night long... His brief smile struck her as a spark ignited but her hot erotic thoughts until she suddenly realized he was referring to the basket she had found on her doorstep. "Oh... oh, yes, thank you!"

"Did you like it?"

"Yes, it was all wonderful, thank you so much..." She was getting so excited she actually had to remind herself what they were talking about.

"Everything was delicious. Did you... did you make it all yourself?"

"No, my hens laid the eggs."

She laughed again nervously. "Well, they were delicious, and so was the spinach, thank you."

"Anything fresh from the ground tastes better."

"I'd love some chickens myself," she declared, at once unnerved and elated because the way they were staring into each other's eyes seemed to have nothing to do with what they were saying. "I've been buying organic eggs for years, but they're nowhere near as flavorful as the ones your hens laid."

"They're good girls, and I spoil them to do death with scratch."

"Scratch?"

"It's what makes the eggs taste so good."

"Really? What's in it?"

"Seeds."

"What kind of seeds?"

"A variety, it all depends on the mix. They're particularly fond of sunflower seeds. Are you looking for Rhode Island Reds?"

"I have no idea, should I be?"

"They're excellent layers. I could build you a coop, if you like, and give you the phone number of a woman in Slaughter who breeds them."

"You would build me a coop?" She couldn't keep the excitement out of her voice. He had just offered to make something for her! Was he merely being a friendly neighbor or was this the rustic equivalent of asking her out? She prayed it was. "That would be wonderful, and it's very nice of you," she added more sedately.

"I only do what I feel like doing, Sofia."

She liked the sound of that so much she couldn't speak for a moment.

"It's important you keep them locked up at night," he warned quietly, "otherwise, they won't survive. There are lots of predators out here."

"Yes, I know, one of them bit me last night," she heard herself confess as she caressed the hair away from her neck. "Do you have any idea what did this?" She showed him her bite mark.

He moved closer.

Beneath her sweater her nipples were so erect they felt electrified as they nearly touched his cold jacket.

"It looks like a vampire bite, Sofia."

"Very funny." She dared to look up at his face. His features were hard... as hard as the hilt of a sword... yet she couldn't grasp how she knew him even though the dangerously exciting knowledge was poised at the very edge of her consciousness... but it wasn't possible, she was only imagining he was the man in her dreams simply because of his goatee and dark hair and because he was wearing leather... black leather like the gloves of the knight who possessed her... "Do you have any hawks?" she said out of the blue.

"Not at the moment. Why do you ask?"

"I was just wondering... So, you have no idea what bit me?"

"I told you."

"Right!" She stepped back. He was scaring her a little by taking deadpan humor to an unnerving extreme, but still she asked, "Did you mean that about building me a coop?"

"I usually say what I mean."

"Well, I would love that... just tell me what you need..."

"I'll take care of it all for you, on one condition."

"Anything," she said without thinking.

"That you invite me to dinner."

"Of course," she promised. 'When... when would you like to come over?"

He walked lightly down the porch steps before turning to face her again, his hands still thrust deep into the pockets of his jacket. "Soon." His first real smile sharpened how handsome he was even as the whiteness of his teeth made his goatee look even more sinisterly dark. "It's full moon tonight, Sofia." He didn't head back down the gravel drive; he disappeared around the house in the direction of the field where she had seen a bonfire burning her first night here...

She shivered, abruptly feeling the cold. The sun was just dipping below the horizon as she picked up her book and hurried inside. It wasn't until later that night, when she was pouring herself a glass of wine, that she realized how inconceivably rude she had been by not even asking him his name.

Chapter Seven

Sofia kept as busy as possible. She unpacked all the candles in her possession and arranged them in the bathroom, creating cathedral-like tiers of wax columns in every shape, size and color. She lined them up across the black marble counter and erected a wax army on two edges of the lion-pawed tub. She felt as though she was in church lighting a flame in honor of all the souls she loved who had moved on, except for the fact that she was completely naked. Only two people she had been close to were dead, but dozens of spirits claimed one wick after the other as she filled the dark bathroom with men and women she had never met and yet which she mysteriously missed anyway as she shivered in her lonely flesh. She had turned down the heat and her breasts and nipples looked carved from rosy marble in the flickering illumination. She had also turned off all the lights in the house, transforming the bathroom into a sacred shrine dominated by the altar-like tub with its animal paws. She was possessed by the need for intense sensual stimulus and contrasts this evening. She deliberately took off all her clothes before she began lighting the candles in order to fully experience the cold, perversely enjoying the way it harvested hundreds of goose bumps on her warm skin like the neat bundles of hay she had seen spread across open fields as she drove back from the city today. All the thoughts corralled in her head depended on the complex landscape of her incarnation; all the parts of her body growing and working together to sustain her sense of self as her soul lorded it over everything in a metaphorical castle of dark desires and lofty hopes.

When all the candles were lit she passionately hugged herself, shivering. It turned her on to sense the subtly warm lick of each little burning tongue as she closed her eyes and concentrated on the sensation. Behind her eyelids she saw candles burning on a stone altar and men and women in beautifully rich clothing... they were being brutally murdered, heartlessly run through with swords where they had sought refuge inside a church powerless to protect them because it was the earthly representative of God who had ordered their deaths...

She opened her eyes and turned eagerly, desperately, towards the hot water. She was so cold... as cold as one of the bodies, stripped of its finery, lying across the stone floor miraculously picking itself up and finding sanctuary in the gloriously warm ocean of another woman's womb... The tub was full. She turned off the tap. The old pipes stopped whining like dogs crying to be let inside and she was plunged into a sepulchral silence that truly made the bathroom feel like a small chapel in the forest's living cathedral. She raised her leg and dipped a cautious toe into the water. It was hot, almost painfully so, but that was just what she craved tonight – violent sensual contrasts that rooted her deliciously in her body. She gradually lowered herself into the bath, whimpering as her chilled flesh seemed to dissolve in the steaming liquid. She slipped beneath the surface with excruciating slowness, but once her hips were submerged the pain was suddenly alchemized into a feeling of fulfillment so intense that she cried out as if in ecstasy, and swiftly sank all the way down to her chin. The tub was unyieldingly hard against her bones... a flooded sarcophagus over which her face floated with its eyes blissfully closed like a painted funeral mask... a marble bath in ancient Rome full of healing thermal waters rising up from the center of the earth... a stone altar where she was being baptized to a whole new life in which she never took the magical dimension of her senses for granted...

She was possessed by strangely vivid images and feelings, and they were all made possible by the man she had caught sitting in her chair reading her book that afternoon, the man who had left her a wicker basket full of small but vital sensual pleasures. She didn't know his name, only that he was apparently her closest neighbor despite the fact that she couldn't see where he lived. The most important thing about him could not be explained. *I know him in my bones,* she kept thinking, writhing restlessly in the tub trying to understand, and remembering the definition of "marrow" she had looked up earlier that evening:

> *A soft, highly vascular modified connective tissue that occupies the cavities of most bones; the substance of the spinal cord; the choicest of food; the seat of animal vigor: the inmost, best or essential part: CORE."*

Yes, she could say without doubt that she knew this man in the very marrow of her bones. Every pore in her skin penetrated and filled with heat, she thought languidly, *Marrow... Marry: to unite in close and usually permanent relation...* Language was a fascinating thing, it was why she loved verse, because the best poerty made use of each word in such a way that all its meanings could come into play and seduce the brain into believing in the eternal mystery of everything...

She remained immersed in the bath until the bracing heat relaxed its hold and the water gradually began growing cold. She was reluctant to leave her sensual candle lit little cathedral, but it was time for communion. Dinner tonight would consist of a hot loaf of bread and a glass or two of red wine. She really wasn't hungry, but she needed to eat something because she definitely wanted to drink. She had a freezer full of organic entrees, one of which she could always microwave later if she wanted, but right now all she felt like doing was thinking about the sexy stranger she couldn't believe was actually her neighbor.

She stood for a timeless while with a lavender towel wrapped around her staring into the vigorous flame rising from a blood-red pillar candle. The more she went over their brief conversation in her head, the less she could believe it had actually happened. After her conventional lunch date, and all the politically correct topics they had pecked at like chickens, the few exquisitely tense minutes she spent on the porch with a man dressed all in black felt like encountering a wolf. The unexpected sight of him sitting in her chair reading a book that meant so much to her *had* frightened her, and part of her remained nervous the whole time they were talking because it was unsettling to have her dreams so casually made flesh. She kept wondering what he had thought of her. He couldn't have known the reason why she was so foolishly tongue-tied in his presence, but he seemed to admire her taste in poetry; at least she had that going for her in his eyes... His eyes!

Clutching the towel tightly around her, Sofia walked through the dark house into her favorite room. Before she ran the bath she piled a generous amount of kindling in the fireplace beneath three split logs, so all she had to do now was set a match to it. Tongues of flame eagerly licked the branches, hungrily growing in strength. She knelt on the cold hearthstones and spread open her towel like violet wings on either side of her naked body. The dry, caressing heat of the fire was very different from the embracing warmth of the water, but they were both delicious in their own way. Fire and water were the core elements of most ancient religious rites, and even Catholic priests lit candles on an altar and sprinkled their parishioners with holy water. She had gone without sex for less than a month, and already her libido was out of control. She couldn't seem to tell the difference between her erotic desires and her metaphysical sensibilities. Yet if she wanted to develop a friendship with her neighbor which might grow into something else, she had to see him for who he was; she had to distinguish him from the fantasy figure who was really only a part of herself and the intriguing subterranean realm of her subconscious.

When her knees began to protest and the fire grew too hot, she returned to the present by turning on the lamp in her bedroom so she could get dressed. She slipped into her favorite black cotton pajama pants, sweater and slippers, and then began blowing out the candles in the bathroom one by one. By the time she finished she was lightheaded, and even more confused by her encounter this afternoon. This man was in no way typical of Clinton; he was not from around here, she could tell that from the way he spoke and just by looking at him. Even though he didn't have an accent she could discern, she imagined there was a European aura about him. His features were strikingly distinct, almost hawk-like, yet there was a softening sensual curve to his firm mouth, and his eyes were large, dark and hooded, slightly evocative of Medieval paintings. His goatee was so thin it looked like a line drawn in ink around his lips, accentuating the strength of his jaw, and she sensed his hair would have been sleek, almost luxurious, if he hadn't apparently taken a pair of scissors to it himself in a fit of impatience… or penance…

She kept busy, toasting half a loaf of French bread in the oven while inexplicably vivid images kept invading her mind and exciting her imagination. Solitude was getting to her, she concluded, unhinging the normal control she possessed over her moods and daydreams. She opened a bottle of Merlot feeling it was too cold for Chardonnay. The gloves all the men in her dream were wearing had her thinking about the Dark Ages and Medieval Europe. The dream itself was undoubtedly inspired by the peasant songs she was writing a paper on, poems that felt much more hauntingly significant out in the country than they had in the city. It would probably be a good idea to read something lighter for a while, she wasn't in any rush to publish, but she didn't feel like reading anything else right now. She loved those lute player songs more and more, especially now that the man she somehow knew in the very marrow of her bones had held the book in his hands and confirmed that they were indeed beautiful...

She sat cross legged on the floor in front of the fire sipping wine and chewing on hot, lavishly buttered bread. The deeper she stared at the sensually writhing flames, the more intensely agile and inspired the dance between her thoughts and feelings became until anything seemed possible. The tangle of kindling had become a smoldering red bed that kept the denser logs burning... her thoughts were like that kindling, intersecting and going off an their own tangents, nothing seeming to make any unified sense until they all suddenly came together in a flash of intuition that ignited more and more associations, the ponderous weight of her reason succumbing to the undeniably passionate feelings surrounding it. She felt whole inside sitting in front of a good fire, body and soul warmed by the knowledge that everything was sensually part of everything else, and that given time she might one day be able to solve the haunting puzzle of her desires and perceptions...

She *had* to stop thinking about her neighbor. God only knew how long it would be before she saw him again; she was going to drive herself crazy obsessing about him. She needed to get some work done, not just fool around on match.com. Her hotmail inbox was probably flooded, but she didn't care; she had no desire to check her e-mails. Her computer was off, her desk dark as a grave, and she kept hearing his quietly deep voice saying, *It looks like a vampire bite, Sofia...* She wondered why such a trite joke was turning her on so much, and why she didn't think less of him for covering up his ignorance by teasing her like that. Obviously, he didn't have a clue what had bitten her so he had fun with her, a very typical guy thing to do. If she hadn't been so busy confusing him with her fantasy man, she might have been annoyed that he didn't seem to realize how worried she was about that bite, which was why she showed it to him... Wasn't it?...

"Oh, God, *stop!*" she exclaimed out loud. *There's no way you're going to make sense of this*, she went on in her head because the sound of her voice in the silent house was uncanny. *All you can do is wait until you see him again.* Until then, her fantasies and his reality were inextricably linked inside her, especially in the witch's brew of her pussy juices as the mere thought of him stoked how inexplicably aroused she was. She wanted him, and she wanted the man in her dream, and masturbating wasn't going to soothe her painfully deepening need. Normally she had much more control over herself, but whenever she thought about him (which seemed to be whenever her heart beat) the last thing she wanted was control over anything, especially of herself and her body. She was haunted by the memory of his voice saying, *I'll take care of it all for you* as though he was promising her much more than a chicken coop.

* * *

The moon was full, but it was still nearly impossible for her to see anything beneath the trees. Running was a waste of breath and effort; all she did was stumble and fall and squander precious time picking herself up off the uneven ground. Brambles seemed to covet the gilded embroidery on her heavy skirt. More than once she had to rip the dress she loved so much in order to free herself from an invisible but tenacious embrace. She had fled immediately after sunset, when the moon was rising in the east. She had been running for what felt like her whole life, not merely a few hours. She desperately needed the moon to see by, but it could also betray her. Praise be, she still did not hear the dreaded sound of pursuit behind her. Nevertheless, she was trapped in the powerful embrace of Rex Mundi, the mountains full of embodied evils that could easily kill her, but the only animals she feared tonight were noblemen with bloody crucifixes embroidered on their tunics. Her father and brothers and uncles were all dead, she knew this even though she could not bring herself to admit it yet. The steep terrain littered with rocks made her stumbling progress through the dark even more perilous. She had long since lost her cloak, but she had ceased to feel the cold. She was bare-headed, and her long hair attracted much covetous attention from the hungry winter trees.

When at last she reached the clearing she had sought for so long, her bones seemed to age a century in the blink of an eye as she sank to the ground. She suddenly felt as light and invulnerable to fear as a skeleton, her heavy gown a shroud she longed to fling off so she could be born again with a different fate entirely. Her ringed hands would take root deep in the earth as her soul slipped into the curled fist of an innocent baby safely surrounded by love. She believed she was ready to die until she heard the unmistakable sound of hoof beats in the darkness, and a second later the smell of sweating horseflesh filled her nostrils. One of her pursuers must have found the hidden path. She picked herself up again, raising her skirt above her knees, forgetting all modesty. Moonlight spilled across the glade, cutting shadows sharper than the swords she was much more afraid of than the peaceful grave. Being murdered by a soldier of the Pope was far worse than dying naturally in childbirth or of sickness and old age. She ran away from the sounds of a mounted knight, the musical jingle of his harness ringing terrifyingly in her skull, but she was soon out of breath and filled with despair; the urge to surrender to her black destiny became more irresistibly intense with every exhausted step she forced herself to take. Her dress was dark-red, her hair brown, but she knew her pale face and hands were as visible as fragments of the moon fallen to earth. There was no escape for her. She thought of her beloved home amidst the trees, and of her final candlelit bath, as a thundering noise directly behind her told her the embodied storm of the crusader was upon her. She turned to face him, holding her head up defiantly. He reigned his horse to a stop so close to her she felt the leather of his boot against her arm through a tear in her sleeve.

"Sofia!" He leaned down and slipped an arm around her waist. "My love, come!" He lifted her up onto the horse in front of him.

Nothing on earth had ever felt as wonderful as the firm saddle beneath her and his hard chest against her. She rested her cheek gratefully on his shoulder for instant before turning to grasp the pommel as he kicked their mount back into an urgent run. Her helpless flight through the night had been transformed into the very real promise of escape by the power of the man leading them into the cover of darkness beneath the trees as confidently as if he possessed an owl's magical vision. She knew, because he had told her, that he believed men had the power to grasp the soul of creation and make the two Gods one again, and for a few blessed moments she was overwhelmed with faith that he was strong enough to dam the flood of hatred pursuing them. Surrounded by his warm arms and protected by his unyileding body she felt as though nothing could ever harm her...

She shifted restlessly, turning onto her other side in the darkness, clutching a pillow... and wrapping her arms around his neck as he lowered her out of the saddle. The courtyard of the Keep was in an uproar. Dazed by all the torchlight and noise, she closed her eyes...

When she opened them again she was lying on a fur coverlet in a strange room still wearing her torn and grass-stained dress. She was alone, but the castle was under sieged. The sounds that reached her ears were unmistakable even though they were distant and indistinct, muffled by layers of stone and tapestries so she could almost believe they were only the echoes of a terrible dream. A single brazier was burning beside the bed and populating the room with menacing shadows. Then she heard a quiet sound, and a beloved silhouette approached her. The man to whom she had been betrothed since she was nine-years-old reached down and pulled her roughly up into his arms. He held her fiercely against him – pressing her cheek into his chest as though the love in his heart could keep her warm and safe forever – and he did not need to speak for her to understand that all was lost. The swift, steady pace of his pulse almost succeeded in drowning out the sounds of the battle, the final moments of both their lives drumming in her ear. Then a thunderous rumbling beneath their feet made her fear the world was about to open up and devour them.

She pulled away from him. "Please, my lord!" she whispered desperately. She could see two tiny flames burning in his eyes like far away stars. "Please do not let me die a virgin, my lord. Take me before it is too late, and let me die by your hands, I beg you!"

He must have sensed her wish before she even spoke for his gloved hands were already lifting her skirt. She fell weakly back across the bed as a double-edged blade of fear and desire cut straight up between her legs. Soon their souls would be stripped from their flesh, they were as naked as they could possibly be with each other even though they did not remove their clothes, for their time on earth was unraveling too swiftly for that. She could no longer see his eyes or even his face, but the trembling light cast by the brazier gilded his powerful silhouette standing between her legs. He placed her feet on his shoulders and leaned towards her, wrapping the gloved fingers of one hand firmly around her neck as with the other he unsheathed the weapon of his manhood. The pain as he penetrated her would have been blinding if it had not already been so dark in the room and in her soul. The defenselessly soft space between her thighs was rent open in a silent scream of agony as he stabbed her repeatedly. She did not need to close her eyes to see all the knights surrounding the castle, yet she no longer dreaded the thrust of their swords as she seemed to feel them slicing up through her body and her hot blood flowing helplessly.

"Oh, my lord!" she gasped. "Please spare me this misery!"

"Save me a place in heaven, Sofia," he commanded harshly, "or in hell, it matters not, for wherever you go, I shall follow!" He covered her nose and mouth with one hand and with the other intensified the pressure of his thumb and fingers against the gentle pulse in her throat. Almost at once the burning pain ebbed into a delicious warmth deep inside her where she had captured all the wonderful qualities that made him a noble knight – his generosity, his perseverance, his pride, his love of beauty. She experienced all his profound sensibilities as a wondrous sensation embodied in his erection. Because of him she was beginning to feel the glorious truth of their divinity as he penetrated her violently. She heard him groan as he tightened his gloved fingers remorselessly around her throat. She couldn't resist trying to breathe against the other rough leather gauntlet covering her mouth and nose, but he made it impossible. She was rising above fear and pain as he poured all the strength of his love into possessing her and strangling her to death. Heavenly clouds began muffling her hearing, yet she distinctly heard him breathe, "God forgive me!" before his silhouette merged with the darkness...

She gasped for breath as she sat up in another bed. Moonlight flooding her room cut into her awareness and kept her divided in half. Part of her knew where she was and was very glad to have woken up, but another much deeper part of her, allied with the synapses in her brain that had spun the vivid dream to life, burned with despair not to find herself in that other room somewhere. Then suddenly she remembered that he was here – that he had followed her and found her just as he had promised he would – and a surge of joy made her feel whole again.

Chapter Eight

It was a radiant day outside, but Sofia deliberately ignored it in an effort to get some work done. She was on sabbatical, she was under no great pressure to publish another paper, but that didn't matter, she simply had to do something to stop thinking about her latest dream. The man who had fatally cut off her breath as he took her virginity was *not* her nice, down-to-earth neighbor, he existed only in her head, and if she didn't get a grip on herself she would end up driving into Baton Rouge two or three times a week to see a psychiatrist.

She spent the morning on the computer even though it literally hurt not to be outside on the porch basking in the beauty of the day. She could sense the sap rising in the trees aching to burst forth as fresh young leaves... just as her every nerve-end felt possessed by a similar restless need and desire to open up and absorb the penetrating power of the sun... of the man who had exerted all the physical and emotional powers he possessed to fulfill her final wish to die by his hand...

Her fingers flew across the keyboard, but no matter how fast she typed she couldn't escape the longing to see him and be with him, to trace the lines of his face with her fingertips in reverent wonder that he had taken flesh again and somehow found her... She tormented herself by trying to imagine the slightly rough, cool feel of his goatee against her skin contrasted by the tenderness of his lips and the warmth of his breath as he kissed her...

She couldn't believe she hadn't asked him for his phone number (not to mention his name) so she could call him and invite him to dinner that very night. It was torture not knowing when she would see him again. He had promised it would be soon, but she had no idea what that meant to him.

Moaning in frustration, she concentrated on copying a poem without making any mistakes.

SONG OF THE DAGGER*

...Did I but heed my dagger, now at night-time,
I should go find thee, love.

Beneath thy shift I should seek out so deftly
The spot where beats thy heart,
And pour thy blood's red warmth out for my dagger,
Because thy kiss, O love, thou hast denied me,
And because I for that thy kiss have thirsted,
Even as the dagger thirsteth for thy blood.

Then will the sunshine sparkle and be merry,
Seeing thy red young blood,
Yea, and the merry sunbeams, they shall dry it,
Together with my tears.
My tears and thy blood shall flow together,
Mingling like rivers twain;
And though thy blood be hot, yet can it never
Be burning as my tears.
Nay, but thy blood will wonder when it feeleth
How burning are my tears...

She sat back in her chair, staring at the violent verses she had just so lovingly transcribed. This dark, kinky streak had always been inside her, she realized that now, but she had kept it safely hidden in a small corner of her libido, only taking it out now and then to play harmless erotic games with Steve on Sundays, which is what they did instead of go to church. The emotional earthquake of Robert's fatal heart attack coupled with the sudden death of her relationship had cracked open this deeply buried violent streak in her sensuality.

Desires and inclinations formerly condemned to the shadows of her subconscious were all pouring like bats out of a cave into the conscious light of day. She was torn between rationally ignoring her vivid erotic dreams and passionately indulging them. She really had to make an effort to forge calm, neutral ground inside herself from which she could attempt to analyze exactly what was going on with her feelings. She needed someone to talk to, but the only person around was a man whose name she didn't even know – a man who looked so much like the knight in her dreams that the line between reality and fantasies was beginning to slip in such an intensely desirable way she couldn't manage to feel afraid.

She wasn't getting any work done on her paper. At around three o'clock she finally gave up and began surfing the web, searching for something, she wasn't sure what. All morning part of her brain had been piecing together clues from her dream, and she entered multiple search terms in Google to see what came up. Topping the results was a site called *dragonkeypress*. She clicked on it and read:

The Albigensian Crusade

By Tracy R. Twyman

In the year 1209, the Catholic Church began its first and only crusade against fellow Christian Europeans: a crusade against a group known as "the Cathars"… a heretical Christian sect who believed that one could commune with the True God through the spiritual experience of "Gnosis" - direct knowledge of the divine. They did not believe in the crucifixion or honor the cross. They also believed that the "Jehovah" of the Bible was actually a demiurge, Rex Mundi, the King of the World, who had created the corrupt world of matter in order to entrap men's souls.

The Languedoc region of France was a bastion of Cathar thought, where it had threatened to become the dominant religion. Nearly 30% of all Cathar priests were drawn from Languedoc nobility, and even non-Cathars in the region usually maintained a cold attitude towards the Church of Rome. The Languedoc was at that time an independent principality, with a distinct culture of esoteric thought and higher learning. So when the "Albigensian crusade", as it came to be called, began, even many non-Cathar locals defended their home-grown heretics to the death.

For the next forty years, the Church attempted to wipe out the Albigensian menace. The destruction of Catharism, which tended to run in families, was so complete that the Crusade is now considered by historians to be Europe's first genocide. Those who weren't killed in the fighting were arrested and tortured by the Dominican Order's Holy Inquisition. The Church's army spared no one, not even non-Cathars, who stood in the way of their stated goal. When Pope Innocent III was asked how the soldiers should know the heretics from the true Christians, he responded with the oft-quoted line, "Kill them all. God will know His own." And that they did. The Cathars and their defenders fought bravely, but in the end it was no use.

Oh, my God, she thought, and quickly searched for more information on this barbaric crusade she vaguely remembered reading briefly about in European History class. Some websites went into interesting depth on the beliefs of the Cathars, but it was one detail that made her gasp out loud. The knights who took up this unholy crusade were distinguished by the red crucifixes they wore on their tunics, not to be confused with the white tunic and differently shaped red cross of the Knights Templar. She couldn't believe her eyes, but it was right there in black-and-white in front of her – her violently sensual dream could really have happened.

* * *

By six o'clock Sofia couldn't stand being inside any longer. The sun was setting between the trees on the western side of the house, but she headed east into the darkening woods. The evening was almost balmy, which felt wonderful and yet was disappointing because it meant she might not need to light a fire later, and the vigorous flames kept her such good company she felt bereft without them. The steady vibration of countless crickets helped soothe her by providing an audio expression of her sensual tension. Unless it was bitterly cold, it was never completely silent in the forest. She glanced over her shoulder and caught a glimpse of the sun's brilliant orange sphere swiftly descending. Brief as it was, twilight had always been her favorite time of day, especially when golden rays pouring between the dark trees made it easy to believe the world was an enchanted place. All her life she had enjoyed vivid, colorful dreams full of people she didn't know, but none of her nocturnal adventures had ever felt as real as the ones she had experienced in her new fairytale bed. It seemed she was taking her sabbatical literally by celebrating her own intimate

Sabbath as she explored the mysteries of her subconscious in a way she had never had the time, space or energy to do before. She paused on the path, her pulse accelerating when she suddenly spotted the silhouette of a person standing just a few feet away. A second later she laughed self-consciously when she recognized her own shadow cast by the sun on the smooth grey-black trunk. She held out a hand, splaying her fingers open to study them in fascination. Everything, including all her wicked erotic thoughts, had come from an absolute darkness. She had never been able to wrap her brain around this fact. Everything from nothingness made absolutely no sense. Or was nothingness latently everything? She kept walking, trying to get away from fruitless metaphysical speculations; the evening was too beautiful to waste locked up in her brain.

She emerged into the open area she had been seeking. Night was quickly falling beneath the trees, but her neighbor's open pasture was flooded with a soft and utterly lovely light. Then another site made her gasp out loud – the moon rising. She had seen countless movies in which the moon looked as big as that, but this felt very different simply because it was real, occupying the same space as her body. Even though it had technically been full the night before, the moon was still perfectly round and a lovely, buttery-white that made her hunger for more ordinary yet totally magical moments like this in her life. Living through all the different seasons in the country was going to be wonderfully different from enduring them in a city, and in that moment she made the conscious decision never to return to Baton Rouge. She would think about what that meant for her position at LSU later, but the truth was that she was tired of writing academic papers about poems written centuries ago by other souls. She was feeling the need to create something of her own, verses that might be able to express – and perhaps help her understand – the exciting relationship between dreams and so-called reality, something she believed in more than ever surrounded by nature's relentless sensuality instead of concrete buildings.

She was very glad she had obeyed the impulse to leave the house and go for a walk just in time to catch the moon poised directly above the horizon. She was amazed by its size and by how it looked almost close enough to touch. It was rising directly across from the setting sun – a cool and beautiful queen ascending to the throne after the blazingly noble death of her lord. She could understand why, to most ancient sensibilities, the earth's devoted satellite was considered feminine. The moon was smooth and curved yet also latently dark, full of unplumbed depths just like a woman, her surface flesh reflecting the sun's light just as she, personally, never stopped thinking about men. It was true that ever since she could remember Sofia had been in love with boys.

She looked back out across her neighbor's field wondering where he was, and could scarcely believe it when she saw him. She knew right away it was him even though he was only a tall silhouette forged by the dying light. She glanced down at the loose white cotton housedress she was wearing that fell just below her knees that made it so easy to believe she had slipped into her dream as she began walking quickly towards him, only this time there *was* a fence in her way. She stared at in consternation, seeing it as a symbol of the rational limits she passionately sought to defy. She watched, penned in by barbed wire, as he unfolded something almost as tall as he was, an object with long, slender legs that formed a pyramid shape... a telescope. His back was to the dying sun as he pointed the instrument at the rising moon.

"Hello!" she called, raising her arm and waving to get his attention. The breeze was growing chillier by the second, but at least it served to carry her voice to him. She couldn't see his eyes, but she felt the touch of his awareness when he turned his head. He did not answer her greeting as he approached her, leaving the telescope behind.

His voice insinuated itself into her bloodstream almost before it reached her ears. "Good evening, Sofia."

"Good evening! Please, tell me your name. I'm so sorry, I forgot to ask you yesterday."

"What's in a name?" he teased soberly.

"You're a man, not a rose," she parried happily. "Or should I just call you 'my lord'?" The blood rushing through her head in astonished embarrassment at what she had just said drowned out the sound of the crickets. For a moment the silence felt terrible as it suddenly grew too dark for her to see his expression.

The crickets began singing again as he said mildly, "If you like. But just so you know, my name is John."

"It's a pleasure to meet you, John." How casual she sounded made her feel she was lying to him. "You have a telescope," she observed inanely.

"I do. Would you care to join me in a little stargazing?"

"I would love that, but..." She glanced down at the wicked looking metal fence. "Do you know where the gate is?"

"Yes, but it's far. I can help you across."

"I don't know…" She couldn't tell him the main reason for her hesitation was the fact that she wasn't wearing any panties.

He leapt over the thorny barrier, and just like in her dream she felt time and space mysteriously collapse as her knees bent and her arms slipped around his neck when he swept her up into his arms. She half cried out, half laughed, "What are you doing?!" even as he set her safely down on the other side of the fence and lifted himself over it again.

"Come, Sofia. Let me show you some stars." He took one of her hands, and all her thoughts seemed to forge themselves contentedly into the warm strength of his fingers. A silly "Okay" welled up inside her like a bubble she popped before it could take shape in her vocal cords and shame her; it wasn't a reverent enough response to the small yet vast gift he was offering her. "Yes, my lord" perched on the tip of her tongue like a butterfly aching to break free of the confining cocoon of her reason, but she said nothing at all as he led her across the grass to his telescope. The moon was higher in the sky but still large and growing brighter, her craters more distinctly etched as the wind picked up and sighed away the last of the daylight up into a sky coming alive with stars.

"You must be cold," he observed, and before she could say anything he slipped out of his jacket and draped the heavy leather over her bare shoulders.

"Thank you, John." It wasn't so dark yet that she couldn't be affected by the sight of his muscular arms in the short-sleeved black shirt he was wearing over his black jeans. "But now *you'll* be cold."

"I'll be fine."

She wasn't about to argue with this traditional male testament to invulnerability, an arrogant assurance that made her smile because she was more than ready to believe it about him. When Steve had said "I'll be fine" it usually meant he didn't care one way or the other what he felt, but she sensed this was not true about John at all.

"It'll take me a minute to get it set up," he told her.

She didn't say anything, succumbing to the profound contentment enfolding her in the shape of the black leather that had only a few seconds ago rested against his warm skin. As night completely possessed the world the memory of her dream became even more vivid; more than ever she felt as though the violent events had occurred only yesterday and not centuries ago, and certainly not merely in her subconscious. She was going to tell him about her dreams, she knew that now, she felt the weight of this responsibility on her shoulders as she exulted in the jacket he had draped across them – something that was part of him and of his own comfort casually yet significantly sacrificed for hers. But she couldn't tell him now; she couldn't yet bring herself to speak to him about something so impossible even though it seemed like the right place to do it out here in the dark beneath the stars. "I would love it if you would come over for dinner tomorrow night, John."

"What's wrong with tonight?"

"Nothing at all!" She laughed. "Except that I haven't had time to cook anything. But that doesn't matter," she added quickly. "I bought an assortment of gourmet cheeses yesterday, and I've got some smoked trout and some smoked salmon, too, if you don't mind a casual meal."

"It sounds wonderful. Come here."

She took his place behind the telescope. She bent over, closing her left eye as she concentrated on placing her right eye over the viewfinder. Her flickering lashes brushed it and for a few seconds all she could discern was a trembling pinpoint of light that slowly came into focus.

"Can you see?" he whispered.

"Oh, yes…" Saturn and its rings were glowing in the darkness of the universe and of her pupil, the most sublime colors imaginable all casually vibrating in her visual cortex. She had seen countless photographs of Saturn in magazines and books, but there was nothing like feeling her body occupying the same space with this unimaginably faraway place. "It's beautiful!" she exclaimed.

"Yes, it is," he agreed, "but not as beautiful as what I'm looking at."

She glanced at him even though it was impossible to see his face. She almost didn't let herself believe he meant what she hoped he did, yet the possibility excited her so much she had no idea what to say. She stepped back so he could slip between her body and the telescope. She was standing so close to him the warm aura of his strength turned his heavy jacket into a burden as she suddenly almost felt weak in the knees with the need to touch him, but she didn't dare, afraid he might think less of her for it. She didn't want him to imagine she threw herself at all men so quickly.

"Now look at this," he urged. "Aren't they amazing?"

She smiled and bent over the viewfinder again. "Oh!" The moon was right there, really close enough to touch this time; all she had to do was reach out and her fingertips would caress the luminously pockmarked flesh, craters so vast and deep they appeared impenetrably black. "This is a great telescope!"

"Sofia..."

She immediately straightened up and turned to face his silhouette, looking expectantly up at his dark face. His eyes were just barely visible as their glimmering depths reflected the stars. She held her breath because he was about to say something important, she could sense it, and she wanted to hear it more than anything... some recognition on his part that echoed her own mysterious certainty they were not strangers to each other at all...

"How is it that you're all alone out here, Sofia? The house was empty for years, then suddenly one day you appeared and I thought I was dreaming."

"Dreaming?" she echoed hopefully.

"Yes..."

"The reason I acted so strangely yesterday, John, was because... because you looked so familiar to me," she confessed as much as she could. "Do you know what I mean?"

"Yes, and no. I want you to tell me about it. When we're finished here, I'll walk you home and go get us a bottle of wine."

"Oh, you don't have to do that, I have plenty of wine." She couldn't bear to let him out of her sight again, not so soon.

Abruptly, he pushed his jacket off her shoulders, gripped both her arms and kissed her, his fingers digging possessively, almost cruelly, into her skin as he forced her mouth open beneath his without any tender preliminaries.

Chapter Nine

THE MOON*

The moon, she fears the sunshine sore,
Because the sunshine knows full well
Wherefore the moonlight is so pale.
The moon is loth that the sun should tell

Her secret; and she hides away
When the sun comes forth, that so, perchance,
The sunshine may forget.
But I am brother to the sun,
He telleth me his secrets all—
How he hath taught the birds to sing,
The ears of corn to turn to gold,
The forests to grow green.
And thus he hath betrayed to me
Wherefore the moon is pale.
The moon, she is a maiden's heart,
And love once dwelt therein,
Ah, in those days the maiden's heart
Was sunshine through and through,
But when love left the maiden's heart,
'Twas then that it grew pale.
And Heaven took it up on high,
Yet sadly still it looketh down
Upon the earth, where love did dwell,
And paler grows the while.

The moon, she fears the sunshine sore,
Because the sunshine knows full well
Wherefore the moonlight is so pale,

The rivers say when she appears:
"O little maid's pale heart,
Come, rest in us!" and in their sleep
The birds all say to her:
"Come, go to sleep in our nests with us!
The grave saith: "Maiden's heart,
Pale heart, make me grow paler too!"
And everything to slumber turns
That so that heart may sleep.
Yet though she see them slumb'ring all,
She slumbers not, nor nods her head,
But stands and watches Sleep.

"That was beautiful," he said when she finished reading the song and put the book down.

"Do you really think so?" she asked shyly.

"I wouldn't say so if I didn't."

"I'm sorry…"

"For what?"

"I don't know, John, I'm confused…"

After his brutally thorough kiss out in the field – when his tongue plumbed the depths of her mouth as though his life depended on it, and hers, too – he let go of her just as suddenly. When she didn't protest – when the only sound she made was a small, breathless moan that only seemed to beg for more – he picked up his jacket and draped it over her shoulders again. Then he turned to the telescope, tucked in its legs, and cradled it beneath one arm. "Let's go," he said, resting his hand lightly but commandingly on her back. Now they were here, in her house, sitting on the loveseat in front of the fire he had started while she was arranging a plate of cheese and crackers in the kitchen.

He set his wine glass down on the small table in front of them. "Tell me about it, Sofia."

Not knowing where to begin, she stared into the fire. The flames encouraged her to burn words freely, no matter how cumbersome and inadequate they seemed, and to express her feelings to him no matter how embarrassingly hot they were.

"Sofia..." He reached over and rested a hand on her knee. "You said out in the field that I looked familiar to you, that you felt you knew me."

"Yes," she whispered, trying to concentrate past the warmth of his touch and failing. Across the room her reading lamp was on and by its steady light she could see his eyes, the fire burning in the darkness of his pupils like the reflected flames of the brazier in the dream she remembered so vividly...

"And now you say you're confused," he prompted, removing his hand. "You need to tell me about it."

"I don't know where to begin, John, it's all pretty... pretty intense!"

"Good." He reached for the bottle. "Let's have some more wine."

She obediently held her glass out.

He refilled it almost to the brim.

"That's too much," she protested half-heartedly. "Thank you!"

"We might as well kill it."

"Mm…" She took a hearty sip.

"I feel as though I've known you for a long time, Sofia."

"Really?" A log popped and a spark flew into the room that landed harmlessly on the stone hearth.

"Why do you sound so surprised?" His eyes commanded her not to look away. "You feel the same."

"Yes, but… it's more than a feeling, actually… You see, I've had some dreams…"

"You don't know anything about me," he spoke slowly, cupping his glass like a chalice between his knees as he stared down into it, "yet already you're telling me I'm the man of your dreams?" His eyes were so penetratingly serious when he turned his head and looked at her again that not even the fire's flickering illumination could help her imagine there was a smile on his lips. In fact, his mouth looked so hard she caught her breath, afraid of she knew not what, and of everything, all at once.

"That's not what I'm saying, Please don't tease me, John."

"Do you really feel I'm teasing you?"

"I don't know… I mean, I really don't know you…"

"You didn't answer my question."

"I *feel* you're not teasing me, John, but my brain can't be so sure."

"Well, I can't say I'm not interested in your brain." He took a sip of wine before staring into its dark depths again. Caressed by firelight, the three-year-old California Merlot was the luminous red of a priceless ruby violently shaped by forces deep in the earth millions of years ago. "I'm listening, Sofia."

She couldn't speak. His profile as he waited intently for her to tell him about her dreams looked so beautiful to her she could hardly breathe as the need to touch him, to kiss him again, to give herself to him completely intensified almost unbearably.

When she didn't say anything he turned his head, and the sternness of his expression as he looked searchingly into her eyes again scared her a little even as it excited her. She leaned forward and carefully set her wine glass down on the table. She could no longer bear to hold its fragile shield over her heart. She longed to expose all her feelings to him. She was aching to show him her very soul, and after what felt like so many centuries, words were too time consuming, too heavy, like all the tombstones littering the dark journey between this peaceful night and that violent one so long ago… She stood up, pulled her dress off over her head, and flung it away. She wasn't wearing anything beneath it, physically he could see all of her now by the fire's flaring light, and it was an intense relief to let her body speak for her silently and eloquently. She watched him set his glass next to hers as his eyes moved slowly from her face to her breasts and down her legs, their intangible yet arousing touch lingering on the smoothly shaved space between her thighs on their way back up. She got up directly in front of him, deliberately letting the flames gild her hair and figure so her beauty shone as brightly as it could for him. Instead of embarrassed or nervous all she felt was an immeasurable glowing pride in who she was.

He stood up, grabbed her by the waist, and pressed the lower half of her body hard against his. "You seem very sure of yourself, Sofia, but this isn't safe.' He ground the hard bulge of his erection into her soft belly. "You know that, don't you."

She was glad it wasn't a question because she couldn't possibly answer. Of course she didn't want him to do anything bad to her and yet, in an inexplicable sense, she did; her heart beat this ultimate paradox more and more urgently the longer she remained submissively silent. She clung to his shoulders, the buckle of his belt biting into her skin, and this sharp little discomfort deepened the dangerous languidness possessing her.

He slipped an arm around her waist and gripped her face, tilting it roughly up towards his. "How can you be sure I'm really you're friendly neighbor, Sofia?" His tone was deliberately sinister. "How do you know you can trust me?"

"Because, I told you... I feel as if I know you *somehow*..."

"Do you?" He let go of her face and thrust his fingers through her hair, getting a firm grip on her head. "Tell me about myself, Sofia. What do you want me to do to you? More importantly, what do you think I *feel* like doing to you?"

The stab of fear she suffered was disturbingly indistinguishable from excitement. "Please, John... please don't make me talk!"

"I'll make you do whatever I want to."

"Yes, please, John..."

His grip tightened excruciatingly on the roots of her hair. "My *lord*'."

Two logs collapsed in the grate and began burning together even more fiercely as the same thing mysteriously happened inside her – his masterful behavior made her so hot that dreams and reality were effortlessly fused in her sex. Her pussy wasn't just wet; she felt hauntingly invulnerable, as if how aroused she was in the dark space between her legs was another dimension where anything was not only possible but desirable.

"I don't know what your dreams are like, Sofia, but I'm warning you," his eyes bored remorselessly into hers, "you're not safe. I've never felt this way, like I could do things to you I've never done to a woman. I'm tempted not to hold back with you, and if you knew me at all, that would seriously concern you."

"I'm not afraid of you, my lord, I can't be…"

"God!" His arm tightened painfully around her. "You're not helping yourself, Sofia."

She held her breath. Crushed against him, his hand firmly gripping her head, his penetrating eyes assumed the dimensions of the universe itself above her. The fire flickering in his black pupils, and in his almost equally dark irises, was the spirit of every star burning in the sky. This was where she belonged, roughly, possessively cradled in his arm, her thoughts indistinguishable from her hair threaded through his fingers. She knew she had risked a dangerous shorthand by stripping, and putting him in a position he could not fully understand since she had not told him a single thing about her dreams. She realized then more clearly than ever how there was a part of her which was much more daring than her cautious reason, and this part of her had wanted to test him, to see if in his blood he too remembered what had happened between them in the past. If she simply described her dreams to him it wouldn't be the same; she would be influencing his perceptions and who he was outside of her own mind. If a few weeks from now, after they had gotten to know each other better, he helped her live out her kinky fantasies, it wouldn't feel the same at all. It was impossible to communicate all of this to him in words, she could only pray her eyes were as eloquent as she longed for them to be as she gazed up at him trustingly. It wasn't just the wine she had drunk that made the fire burning in his eyes read like a language she somehow understood. His body was hard, and with every inch of hers she could feel the dangerous strength in his muscles, she knew she would be wise to be afraid, but she couldn't be, not with his aura also enfolding her. Embraced by his honest energy, which he attempted to make threatening, she felt perfectly, paradoxically safe…

He let go of her so abruptly she stumbled backwards, gasping at how intensely she immediately missed their breathtakingly closeness. She became uncomfortably aware of the heat of the fire caressing her exposed flesh as the distance of a mere few inches between them felt like a chasm she didn't have the power to breach.

"Go to your room, Sofia," he commanded in the tone of an adult punishing a little girl. "And walk slowly, *very* slowly. I want to watch you, and I also want you to have plenty of time to think about the position you've put yourself in with a complete stranger."

She stepped past him, deliberately brushing her arm against his, reassuring herself with the contact. The sensation of her skin caressing his was electric, almost unbearably thrilling because of how much more it promised. She hated losing sight of him; she kept resisting the urge to turn her head and glance over her shoulder to make sure she hadn't only imagined the reality of his presence in her home. It seemed to take forever to reach her bedroom. The house was dark, yet she sensed he had no trouble making out her naked flesh moving before him like the moon obeying its orbit. She thought about how Orpheus must have felt preceding Eurydice out of Hades even as she felt herself drawing closer to a fearlessly hot dimension with every step she took in obedience not only of his command but of the force shaping her dreams. She told herself he was following her, but she had to strain to catch the subtle sound of his boots against the wooden floor because he moved as silently as a cat – as a wolf – behind her.

When she reached the bedroom she walked over to one side of her bed and then stopped, not knowing what to do next and not daring to face him until he told her she could. When nothing happened for nerve-racking seconds, the darkness began pressing against her and she couldn't resist whispering, "My lord?"

"I'm here, Sofia."

She fervently wished there was a brazier she could light as she suddenly, desperately missed the fire. The darkness was so absolute it was like being inside herself. She almost couldn't be sure this wasn't just another dream from which she might awaken alone with no sexy neighbor to look forward to seeing again, and how desolate this possibility made her feel caused her to moan as if in fear.

"Turn around and sit on the edge of the bed." His voice was quiet but absolutely firm, not in the least bit tender or potentially forgiving of her disobedience.

She obeyed him, keeping her back straight and her legs together, her hands resting on her knees as she struggled to distinguish the shape of his body from the night. She wondered where the moon was. It had grown overcast as they drank and talked. Then at last she felt more than saw him move closer.

"There's a lot we have to talk about it, Sofia, but it's too late for words tonight, you've seen to that."

She tensed, afraid he was about to tell her he was leaving.

"Lie back."

A wave of exultation washed over her as once more she did as he said, sinking gratefully back across the feather mattress not just because it felt so good beneath her bones, but because so far he was obeying the choreography of her dreams. She knew it could easily be coincidence – she had taken the first step in the dance herself by standing next to the bed – nevertheless, a hot rush of hope indistinguishable from desire stabbed her directly between the legs. She was about to fuck a complete stranger, an exciting yet inaccurate thought she pushed aside in favor of the much more arousing sense that she was magically embodying time and space as she spread her thighs for him, and then raised her legs around his impenetrable silhouette, the base of her spine dipping over the edge of the bed. She was more than ready for him, yet she still gasped when he roughly gripped both her ankles, straightening her knees as he forced her thighs together and rested the back of her ankles on his shoulders.

"Do you want my cock, Sofia?"

"Yes!" she breathed.

He reached down and slapped her cunt with his hard, open hand.

She cried out more from shock than pain.

He repeated beneath his breath, "*Yes?*"

"Yes, my lord!" She could scarcely believe it, but she knew it was true – this man was going to take her beyond her wildest dreams. A rush of fear mingled with the trepidation tingling in her burning labial lips which told her she should be worried, that she should say something, maybe even beg him not to really hurt her, but she still had no desire to speak. She heard him opening his pants, and she suffered her first real fear as she thought, *What if he doesn't have a big cock?* But that simply wasn't possible, she had felt the bulge in his jeans when he had her pressed up against him; his buried erection had dug into her belly in a way that promised she wouldn't be disappointed.

He leaned into her, forcing her legs down between them as he braced himself on her breasts, crushing them cruelly into her chest beneath his hands. More than one dream was coming true as he pinned her down beneath a delicious mix of fulfillment and anticipation, the friction between the two feelings igniting as a flash of lust in her pelvis. Never before had her hole felt so warm and wet and ready to be penetrated. Absolutely all of her was starved for what was to come, for what she had dreamed about and imagined, but never really experienced in this body trapped now beneath an implacable force taken the form of a man she barely knew and yet wanted more than anything. In those moments the details that had shaped his personality were irrelevant because she was about to get to know him in the truest and deepest sense. Her tender breasts aching in the grip of his hard fingers, the muscles in the backs of her legs beginning to smolder from the strain of the totally vulnerable position he had put her in, she should have been uncomfortable instead of so turned on it made not being able to take a deep breath irrelevant. His shoulders were broad and strong, effortlessly supporting her desire to open herself to him completely. He made her wait just long enough for her to hear everything that wasn't being said between them, and there was no talk of protection. It was dark in the room, and yet her longing for him felt brighter than the fullest moon in the ocean of her blood. When he penetrated her, she made no sound at all; the fulfillment was too intense to express. He lodged his head in the heart of her hole for an excruciatingly suspenseful moment, then he drove his erection into her body with a fierce thrust. Her pussy was tight, the sensation was rending, shocking in its suddenness, and nothing had ever felt better. He groaned, but it was not a vulnerable sound; it was much more a growl of cruel satisfaction as he began fucking her violently. His relentless rhythm made her forget to compare him to her dreams as it drove all the thoughts out of her mind except for one final triumphant firework in her synapses – *Steve never fucked me like this!* At first her only fear was that it couldn't last, that he couldn't possibly sustain that level of energy without getting tired or coming too fast, but this worry soon dissolved as he rammed his hard-on well past her G-spot, mysteriously touching upon the absolute submissiveness of her soul and overwhelming her with a pleasure much more profound than her clitoris could ever give her. He didn't speak to her, not with words; he was telling her everything she needed and wanted to know about him as he banged her with merciless intensity; relentlessly. After a while she gripped one of his wrists, not to take the pressure off her breast but in a passionate effort to move his hand up towards her neck.

As if he sensed what she wanted, he reached up and clutched her throat. "I'm going to come in you," he warned. "I'm going to come so deep inside you, you're going to *breathe* my cum!"

She struggled instinctively, but he was even stronger than the man in her dreams, and apparently more practiced as well. His thumb and fingers pressed against just the right pressure points in her neck to make even thinking about catching her breath impossible. She went perfectly still beneath him as he brought himself to a climax so deep between her thighs it might actually have been the hot rush of his cum filling her lungs as he ejaculated. His own breathing was ragged as he removed the pressure from her throat so she could savor the haunting oxygen of his orgasm filling her body, his cock pulsing in rhythm with her racing heart. His erection was still rampant when he pulled out of her abruptly and slipped her feet off his shoulders.

It was too sudden, she wasn't ready to let go of him even though it was only her pussy that had clung to him, but the endorphin level in her blood had skyrocketed to the point where she was so languid with fulfillment that talking felt more irrelevant than ever. She was aware of the fact that he was closing his pants casually, as if nothing special had happened between them. Suddenly, she sensed it was imperative that he know something of what was happening inside her. She raised herself up on her elbows. "John, I've never…" She didn't quite know how to describe it. "I've never done anything like that before." She was sprawled wantonly before him, her spread legs hanging off the edge of the bed while he remained a self-contained silhouette.

"I told you, it's too late for words tonight, Sofia. Or did you really think I was finished with you? Get up."

She obeyed him at once.

"Turn around and bend over." He didn't touch her, he simply waited for her to do as he said, adding beneath his breath, "God, what a beautiful ass" before he smacked her soft cheeks with such force she nearly fell facedown across the bed.

Being spanked was not new to her, she had asked Steve to do it to her a few times, but this was very different; there was nothing playful or tentative about it. Steve had even stopped himself once, complaining that his hand was starting to hurt, but she knew right away that would never happen with this man.

"Brace yourself," he commanded, and struck her again even harder, his open hand making such vicious contact with her ass it seemed to impact the very bones beneath her burning cheeks.

She cried out in pain, she couldn't help it, but all that truly mattered was that he was still there with her. He grabbed a handful of her hair and forced her head back as he slapped her again with even more terrible strength. He spanked her for so long that by the time he placed a hand between her shoulder blades and pushed her down across the bed she was sobbing beneath her breath. Her ass was on fire, and her sympathetically smoldering sex was so wet she felt her juices trickling down the insides of her legs more swiftly than the sticky warmth of his cum. She deserved to be punished. She should have described her dreams to him when he asked her to, not tested him like this, even though she didn't for one second regret it.

Everything he was doing to her felt much more meaningful and important than words ever could, and the more what he did to her hurt, the more profoundly significant it felt.

"You know why you needed to be punished, don't you, Sofia?"

"Yes, my lord!" she whispered, sniffing back her tears. Her hair was covering her face, but she knew when he sat down beside her as the mattress dipped beneath his weight.

"Listen carefully, Sofia. There's an old oak tree directly behind your house next to the fence. You're going to write your dreams down for me. You're going to tell me everything about them, not holding anything back. Are you listening?"

"Yes, my lord..."

"You'll write them out by hand and put the pages in that oak tree. You'll do this by tomorrow evening before the sun sets. Do you understand?"

"Yes, my lord... but what if it's raining, the paper will get-"

"You heard what I said." He cut her off by spanking her ass again, as a reprimand. "Put them in a plastic bag, do whatever you have to, just make sure your dreams are in that tree before nightfall."

"Yes, my lord," she repeated in growing wonder, and appreciation. She should have realized that writing about her erotic fantasies would be easier than casually trying to talk about them. She felt him get up, and waited for him to say something else, to give her another command, whatever; she was willing to obey him no matter what he told her to do.

She's not sure how much time passed before she suddenly realized the silence behind her was both suspiciously deep and disturbingly empty. She pushed herself up and turned around, sitting on the edge of the bed and quickly looking around before getting up in disbelief. The room was empty. She was the only one there; her heart was the only one beating and giving life to the darkness.

"John?" she called softly, for some reason not daring to raise her voice. She hurried out into the living room, noting the fact that the front door was closed as she prayed he would be sitting on the loveseat waiting for her, but he wasn't, he was gone, and even in the midst of her bitter disappointment she wasn't, for some reason, surprised. Their wine glasses were on the table where they'd left them, and she was inordinately grateful for this evidence that she hadn't only dreamed everything that had just happened. Beautiful red embers glowed beneath a heavy black log that had burned out, and she shuddered, wrapping her arms around herself as she began to feel how cold it was in her house. Most of the cheese she had laid out was still on the plate along with wafer-thin crackers that already looked stale. Her inner thighs were sticky, her ass was burning, and her pussy was smoldering contentedly – there was no doubt he had really been here, but it was still hard to believe because of the way he had simply left without saying goodbye; without holding her tenderly for even a moment while he whispered something – anything – to help her feel good about what had happened. He had left as abruptly as she woke from her dreams. Yet it wasn't true that he had left without promising her anything. He had given her a command she had promised to obey by sunset tomorrow, and anticipating this task was the only thing that would help her sleep even as it kept her awake long into the night.

The Fire in Starlight

Chapter Ten

It was no surprise to Sofia when she awoke to an overcast day. Already she couldn't remember if the weather had affected her as much when she was living in the city as it did out here in the country. She recalls being mildly depressed on rainy days, but there was always so much to do, so much traffic to fight, deadlines to meet, classes to teach, she didn't have time to dwell on her mood. Well, if she truly intended to write some poetry of her own, being hypersensitive to her every thought and feeling is a good thing, or so she hopes.

She lay in bed for as long as she could, but the oppressive heaviness of the atmosphere combined with that of her comforter made her feel restless rather than cozy. She had a task to perform that wasn't going to be easy, but the first thing she intended to do was find that oak tree. She had to make sure it was there, and that there really was a niche in it in which she could place the papers when she was finished with them. She knew there would be, there *had* to be, but a part of her she didn't admire kept dwelling between shame and skepticism on this dreary a.m. She had a pretty good idea what Steve would say about her behavior last night – he would call her a slut and declare he was glad to be rid of her. Fortunately, she was completely indifferent to what he might think. Robert might have understood, but she couldn't be sure since she had never shared this aspect of herself with him, hell, she hadn't even shared it with herself this openly and honestly until recently. The fact that a stranger seemed to understand her better than a man she had known for years ever did was hard to believe, as was the fact that she had loved it when he literally fucked her to within an inch of her life. The conventionally programmed part of her brain was worried she was turning into one of those women the police shook their head over sadly (judgmentally) secretly thinking *she asked for it* when they found her body. Well, technically she hadn't asked for anything; she had not said a word about her kinky fantasies to a man who read her deepest, darkest feelings like an open book. He still didn't know yet how perfectly he had made her dreams come true, but he soon would, once he read what she had to say.

While she was eating breakfast, the sun momentarily broke through the clouds and sent a single shaft of light into the house. She stared at it gratefully, willing it to stay. She gazed entranced by the way it shown off the empty bottle of wine she had shared with John last night, illuminating the dark glass and creating a sparkling little star on the edge of the neck as she turned away and caught it in the corner of her eye. She had cleaned up the cheese and crackers but deliberately left the bottle there to remind her that last night had really happened.

After tea and toast, she slipped on her lavender jacket and stepped outside. The dampness of the air made the cold seep into her bones almost immediately. She didn't need to watch the Weather Channel to know Clinton was experiencing record-low temperatures. She was glad; at least she was assured of a fire's company tonight. She suspected she would not see John again so soon... John, the man she had willingly, slavishly, called "my lord" and allowed to ejaculate inside her without protection while the desire to breathe climaxed violently inside her. It was too soon for her brain to wrap itself around those moments and remember them clearly. Thinking about them made no sense at all, because whatever it was she had felt had transcended the traditional idea of pleasure. The experience had been intensely, violently erotic, frightening and yet cathartic. She could think of even more adjectives, but none of them truly captured the essence of those moments when she should have been terrified for her life but was instead overcome by entirely different feelings.

At first (to her intense shame) she had no idea which of her many trees was an oak. She recognized the Magnolias, of course, and even the Tulip trees because of their big leaves that for some reason reminded her of a cat's face and ears with their pointed tips. She positioned herself at the center of the house and walked forward. There was only one tree it could be which was indeed growing right beside the fence, and she was able to take her first deep breath of the day when she saw the small dark hole in the trunk. She had to stand on tiptoe to see inside it, and she wasn't surprised to discover it was full of ravished acorns. A tentative exploration with one gloved hand proved the space was just deep enough to conceal folded sheets of paper. The discovery made her inordinately happy. She didn't question how he had known about this tree on her side of the fence, the important thing was it was real, which meant *he* was. It seemed ludicrous that she needed so much objective proof of his reality, and this concerned her somewhat, as if part of her mind questioned her own sanity. As she walked back to the house, she wondered what a therapist would say about her situation, probably that grief and loss had unhinged her in some way, and that she was suppressing her sadness by sublimating it into erotic dreams and fantasies she was dangerously projecting on a complete stranger. She was glad Robert's disdain for the psychiatric profession as a whole had rubbed off on her. As lovers of poetry (the darker and more passionate the better) psychoanalysis, he had insisted, was their mortal enemy. If she went to a psychiatrist, he or she would probably prescribe some sort of drug that would numb her into not caring about anything. Far better to live dangerously than not to feel at all.

It took her longer than she had thought it would to write her dreams on the thick, expensive paper she found in the desk Robert had left her. It was the same paper he had written his last letter to her on, a thought that filled her with a morbid anxiety she had trouble dispelling. She had to get up and make herself a cup of Green tea – which she drank standing at the kitchen counter snacking on corn chips and Hummus – before she was able to get back to writing (as neatly as she could with a black pen) on what began to feel like sacred parchment. The paper would be coming full circle when she slipped it back in a tree. One minute she felt like a little girl playing a game with her cute neighbor, and the next like what she truly was – a beautiful, desirable woman defying reasonable safety to communicate with the dangerously exciting man she was falling in love with.

It was difficult to write dispassionately yet descriptively about her powerfully sensual subconscious fantasies, if that's what dreams really were. Since Robert's death, events seemed to be conspiring to force her to define her beliefs. She had always considered herself an agnostic, not sure if there was a God or if the soul was truly eternal or not, but certainly not discounting the possibility. Yet lately (and her love of poetry might have clued her into this) she was wondering if perhaps she wasn't more of a mystic. After all, she was actually considering the possibility that her dreams might be memories of a past life, a concept that struck her as ridiculously New Age. Yet the first thing she had decided as she drove towards Clinton and her new life was that she didn't believe in coincidence. The choreography of events was a fact in her personal experience, which put her squarely in the mystic camp. And how could she not believe in the magic of synchronicity when a man she had just met made her dreams come true without even trying? Although to say he had not made a considerable effort was untrue as it must have taken all the physical strength he possessed to fuck her the way he had. Every time she thought about it, she experienced a rush of heat deep between her legs where some of his virile seed might still be searching for her egg. It was a good thing she hadn't gone off the pill after she left Steve. She was still taking it because it regulated her periods and kept her PMS under control, yet if she had slept with Marcus (God forbid!) she would definitely have made him wear a condom. It wasn't safe to have unprotected sex wih strange men, but that was exactly what she had done last night, and she didn't for one second regret it.

Sofia waited until four o'clock to put the pages with her dreams written on them into the tree trunk. She hadn't placed them their sooner just incase it rained. It made her feel good to know that her feelings had mysteriously become the heart of a tree growing so majestically on her property. She did take the precaution (even though it made the act feel less romantic) of slipping the folded pages into a plastic bag and sealing it tight, because even though she had written her dreams in permanent black ink, it wasn't waterproof. She wondered when he would come for them, and suspected it would be at night, when she couldn't watch him from a window. She had to suppress the thought that the pages might still be there tomorrow morning when she woke up. She had made the decision to trust him, and as a result she had experienced the most fulfilling sex of her life, it didn't matter what anybody else thought about it. Some women liked vanilla, others lived for chocolate, and some (like her, apparently) lived for extremely dark, *dark* chocolate indeed.

A six o'clock it felt like midnight. She turned on the outside lights, thinking he might need them to see by when he came to pick up her dreams. Her porch lights didn't reach that far out into the yard, but she couldn't resist giving him at least a semblance of assistance, not that she thought he needed it. She was on her way to the kitchen, ostensibly to fix herself something to eat even though she wasn't all that hungry, when one of her windows caught her attention. She went and stood close to the glass and laughed out loud, thinking, *Who needs TV when I've got the Discovery Channel right here?* All sorts of nocturnal creatures had been attracted to the lamp shining just inside the window. The biggest were a couple of little green tree frogs that reminded her of the rubber pencil erasers she had loved so much in elementary school. They were stuck to the glass, sitting perfectly motionless except for the pulse beating in their throats as they fed on tiny microscopic insects that flew blindly into their mouths. Around them hovered moths of all different sizes, some strikingly large and lovely in a sinister way, others small enough to be in danger. She gasped in shock when one of the frogs suddenly stretched out its body, flicked its long tongue, and in a flash caught one of the moths, which kept fluttering grotesquely inside it's belly for a few seconds.

"Oh, my God!" she exclaimed. Somehow, witnessing the ruthless drama of the food chain in real life was viscerally different from watching it on the Nature Channel. For an instant it made her want to become a vegetarian, but in the end she couldn't deny her carnivorous kinship with the adorable little stick-um frogs, as she christened them. She stood entertained by this miniature version of the Wild Kingdom for a long time. The life and death drama was riveting, and there was nonstop action to observe. She was also fascinated by the moths. She had never seen one so up close before and she couldn't believe how big and round their pitch-black eyes were. There was one pressed motionless against the glass doing absolutely nothing except soaking up the light coming from her living room, and she was able to study it at leisure. The intricacy of its wings was breathtaking, and it was a little disturbing what a clearly defined face it possessed. She felt something stirring inside her as she gazed at its fierce, scrunched up features. The sensation was strangely urgent, but it wasn't a physical need or hunger. She thought, *Moths looks like the ghosts of warrior princes,* and suddenly she understood the meaning of that feeling which was as subtle and yet as exciting as a light caress against her clitoris, only it wasn't emanating from a bodily organ at all – it was her soul telling her she needed to write a poem.

She walked slowly to her desk, a little in awe of the inspiration, and very afraid it would come to nothing. She had never been pregnant, she didn't know if it felt anything like this – a kindling deep inside her, a mysterious gestation pressing against her perceptions because it was her responsibility to concentrate all her powers on it and bring it to life on a clean sheet of paper. For the second time that day, she sat curled up in her green chair writing by hand. She didn't even remember to pour herself a glass of wine she was so engrossed in the lines flowing from her. When she at last looked up, she was astonished to discover that over an hour had passed and her stomach was grumbling. Now that she had fulfilled a more subtle hunger, an obvious appetite was demanding her attention.

She was smiling as she microwaved a container of organic meat lasagna and poured herself a glass of red wine. For over an hour she had not thought of John and the erotic confessions she had hidden in a tree trunk. She knew Robert would be proud of her. Whether the poem was good or not, it didn't matter; at least she had written one. She couldn't believe it had taken her this long, it seemed inconceivable, but better late than never, she concluded. She let the verses rest, cooling like a metaphorical pie while she ate and drank her wine in front of the fire. Then she sat cross-legged on the hearth stones, picked up the notebook, and read what she had written.

Ode To A Moth

Moths look like the ghosts of warrior princes,
ashes of armor and evanescent cloaks of glory,
burning ideals rewarded by the freedom of flight
resting on my windows desiring the light
determined backs to an eternal night.

Moths have big dark penetrating eyes,
they're much more interesting than butterflies.
Tree frogs dine on my windowpanes at night,
patrons at the restaurant of light,
but even though I tap the glass in warning,

sepia wings and lens-like eyes
leave no imprint in the darkroom of a frog's belly.

It's written on a moth's wings in bas-relief
one story of all the lives composing me
as I die for the night cocooned in violet sheets
confident I will rise again mysteriously.

* * *

In the morning Sofia was doubly elated – she had written her first poem, and the pages she had secreted away in an oak tree were gone. It didn't matter that it hadn't rained yet and that the sky was even more brooding. The brewing storm was indistinguishable from her excitement. It was possible she might see him tonight, and this gave an almost painfully promising edge to every minute of the day. She was too restless to stay inside. Not even the anxious thought that she might miss him if he came by could keep her from slipping on her jacket and gloves and prowling the edges of her property. How unusually cold it was for this time of year energized her.

She set out determined to find the gate linking her land with his, but in places the trees were so dense, and the ground between them so littered with fallen branches that kept snagging on her pants and hair, that she finally gave up. The exertion got her heart pumping fast, which was what she wanted. As soon as it got a little warmer she would start jogging down the gravel road. She hadn't exercised since she left BR, and her muscles were beginning to protest.

She was heading back in the general direction of the house when she heard a sound that made her stop and listen. "What the *hell* was that?" She was reminded of old Hollywood dinosaur movies as she heard the astonishing noise again – a loud, braying bellow she could easily imagine emanating from the throat of a brontosaurus. She changed direction, following the escalating prehistoric cacophony. She emerged from the trees and stopped dead in her tracks again. The field adjoining her property was littered with cows, an entire herd of black, brown and white bovines, some busy spreading out across the lush grass while others were already in their self-allotted spot chewing contentedly. Where she and John had stood the night before last gazing up at the heavens, two golden calves were nudging each other playfully. For a minute she couldn't believe he hadn't even mentioned the fact that he raised cattle as well as chickens, until she remembered that she really didn't know much about him at all. The herd must have wandered here from an adjoining field, which explained why she hadn't seen them until today. What she couldn't explain was why the sight of the healthy-looking cows and big black bulls made her feel so oddly disillusioned. For some reason she was turned off by the thought that her mysterious lover raised beef cattle.

She turned away from the depressingly bucolic sight – which was only an illusion since it probably wouldn't be long before many of those lovely, heavily sensual animals were led to the slaughterhouse – and started in the direction of her mailbox. She wasn't expecting any exciting correspondence, at least not by way of the U.S. postal service, but it was an excuse to stay outside, and it was something to do besides wait for John to suddenly show up again as she fervently hoped he would. She entertained the thought that he might leave a note (perhaps a written command?) in the tree for her, and even though she thought this unlikely, she knew the mere possibility would keep her looking in there regularly.

The red jeep with the flashing lights on top was just pulling up to her box.

"Good morning!" Kelly greeted her cheerfully.

"Good morning!" She smiled, glad to see another human being.

"Here you are." Kelly handed her a small stack of envelopes, all of them bills by the look of them. "It sure is cold out!"

"Yes! Um, excuse me, could I ask you something?"

"Sure."

"My neighbor, the one who lives somewhere back there," she glanced over her shoulder in the general direction of the cow field, "he left a housewarming basket on my porch the other day and I'd really like to thank him. I know he lives by himself, but I don't have his address…"

"Well, I'm not sure who you mean. Over that way's the Patrick property, Frank and Anne Marie Patrick. To the east there's Roger and Stacy Clemens, and Mark and Harriet Rogers live just north of here."

"Oh… okay, thanks."

"If there's anything you need, just leave me a note in the box."

"I will, thank you." Her quiet voice was drowned out by crunching gravel as the jeep made a U-turn and drove off. She didn't notice the walk back to the house, the dark clouds above inseparable from the black despair in her soul. He was married! He had lied to her when he told her his name was John! His real name was Frank!

No, she couldn't believe it. Despite technically irrefutable evidence provided by the government, it just wasn't conceivable that her gloriously sadistic lover was a typical married man cheating on his wife. It was entirely possible that he didn't live across the field at all, that she had simply assumed he did because he had walked away in that direction the evening they met, and because she had seen him there last night. Yet he *had* to live around here somewhere, it was the only way he could have known she had just moved in and brought her a welcome basket.

Only her body was superficially relieved to step inside out of the cold, the rest of her was numb with despair. Her lover was a married man, a *married* man! She cursed herself for prying, for trying to find out where he lived, for not just patiently waiting for him to get in touch with her again. Yet if he *was* married, it was better she found out now, wasn't it, before she fell in love with him? The word "before" struck her soul like a blow. It was far too late to think of "before" when it came to him, there had never been a "before" except in the sense that she had somehow known him before they even met. Oddly enough, in the face of adversity, she was absolutely certain there was nothing wrong with her psychologically; that she wasn't suffering from imaginative delusions. It had felt absolutely right to call him "my lord" just as she had in her dream. She *had* somehow known him before they made love, and she certainly knew him now, no doubt about that, she just didn't have any real facts about him other than the impossible ones provided by the postal service. Instead of a phone number where she could reach the man she was fucking, she had an old oak tree. Before the conversation with her mail carrier, she had considered this romantic, it had made poetic sense; stashing a handwritten "love" letter in a tree was like something out of another century, merging him even more indelibly with the man in her dreams. Yet *was* it romantic, or was it simply the only way he could communicate with her because he was married?

There were no answers to all the agonizing questions suddenly buzzing in her head like a disturbed wasp's nest. If she wasn't going to sit around in a miserable stupor all day she had to stop asking them and just wait, the hardest thing on earth to do.

She took off her jacket and gloves and went into the bathroom. She swept the hair away from her neck. The bite marks were fading, but they were still clearly there. Every night she inspected the bed sheets carefully, and so far nothing else had bitten her, thank God. She glanced at her face, and was pleasantly surprised by how pretty she looked with her cheeks flushed from her brisk walk out in the cold, and with her brown irises glowing like tiger's eyes as the memory of last night kept replaying in the back of her mind no matter what else she was thinking about. She was beautiful, and remembering this made her feel better, not because it appealed to her vanity but because it gave her a glimpse into *his* perspective. Gazing at her reflection, she understood why he was attracted to her, why she had been able to inspire him enough to fuck her the way he had, and why he would want to come back. The possibility that he was married wasn't necessarily the end of the world; there *was* such a thing as a divorce. After all, she had essentially been married herself less than a month ago. She had never cheated on Steve, but she had thought about it more than once, and if she had met John, she didn't doubt for a moment she would have been unfaithful with him. She couldn't judge a man she knew nothing about yet. All she knew for sure was that she needed to see him again, to be with him, to give herself to him no matter how dangerous or forbidden it was.

Chapter Eleven

After the sun had set behind the clouds, Sofia poured herself a glass of wine, sat down at the computer, logged onto the Internet, and deleted her profile on match.com. With a grim smile on her face, she ignored the appalled screams of protest issuing from a part of her brain that insisted she was cutting herself off from the world and perilously throwing herself into the arms of a potentially married man. Deleting her profile online was an act of rational suicide that felt wonderful to her soul. It was an act of faith; the first cut of a sword defending her intensifying belief in something other than what the small part of her brain she was using could clearly understand. At all cost she would defend her feelings and intuition no matter how lost she might appear to be in fantasies and dreams with no bearing on reality. That was no longer even the case; she had received stunning proof John was someone she definitely wanted to get to know whether they had been together in a past life or not. He had fucked her the way she had always dreamed of being fucked.

He's not married, she thought. *He's not married. He's not married!* Her mission accomplished, she deliberately ignored all the messages in her hotmail inbox and shut off the computer. She went and sat on the loveseat in front of the fire. She wasn't really conscious of the fact that she was crying until she felt salty tears cynically scalding her cheeks, surprising her, because deep down she was feeling very positive. This was her punishment for trying to find out more about John by way of a third-party who couldn't possibly know him as she already did. Her dreams were in his hands now and she was possessed by a growing excitement – by faith that he was man enough to make them come true. The book of Romanian Lute Player songs was sitting on the table in front of her. She reached out and flipped it open.

Alone*

Beside the fire thou toldest me

Some tale, and thou didst watch the fire,
That so thou might'st not see my tears.
Into the fire my tears flowed down,
Then to the tears thus spake the fire:
"And would ye quench me?"

There was a rumble of thunder. She sat up alertly, listening beyond the crackling of the fire for another sign that the storm which had been brewing for two days had finally arrived. The atmosphere might get some relief even if she didn't... yes, there it was again, the deep, heavenly groan caused by phallic lightning flashes in the distance...

As if obeying a cosmic cue, she took her wine glass into the bedroom, set it down on the nightstand, and began undressing. She sensed in her blood that he wouldn't make her wait another night for him. She was no longer listening to her mind, which was always annoyingly reminding her that she could be wrong about everything. The poem she had written had given her soul a haunting boost of confidence and centered her in a much deeper part of herself which knew things without understanding how; a part of her that didn't for one instant doubt in the veracity of her perceptions even though she could not prove her conclusions in any rational court of law.

She switched the bedside lamp to its dimmest setting. Despite the fact that the heat was turned down and it was quite cold in her house except for around the fireplace, she stripped off her layers of clothes standing in front of the French doors. Thunder drummed again overhead and she allowed herself to be possessed by the arousing sense that she was on display. He could be out there looking in on her, watching her figure gilded by the light as she slipped slowly out of her black leggings. Her cozy white socks went next, followed by a gray sweater and the black T-shirt she was wearing beneath it. Only her black bikini panties remained, and she deliberately kept them on as she walked back to the fire to warm herself up for a minute before quickly returning to the bedroom as if he was actually there waiting for her.

Once more facing the French doors, she slipped her panties down her legs, stepping out of them gracefully and kicking them aside disdainfully. She was so cold her skin clung tautly to her bones. Her nipples ached they were so hard as she pressed her breasts against the glass, straining to see out into the night. She didn't turn on the outside lights to better appreciate the drama of the storm, and she was rewarded by a vivid flare that illuminated the open field beyond her trees. The almost simultaneous roar of thunder was so loud she slapped her palms against the glass to brace herself. She held her breath until lightning struck again, gasping with pleasure as the silver light imprinted the silhouettes of trees on her retinas, and the inescapable rumbling of the atmosphere crashed through her brain in an audio landslide, sweeping all annoying thoughts away by completely rooting her in her receptive senses. The wind had picked up and was working its way through the forest in caressing gusts made even more hauntingly urgent by the formless power behind them. She could hear the agitated rustling of Magnolia branches through the glass. Logic said he wouldn't show up on a night like this, yet with every explosive flash she experienced a stab of excitement that made it clear her body felt otherwise. She was so turned on by the violently sensual spectacle of the storm, combined with the possibility that the man she called "my lord" might actually enter her home again soon, that she kept having to resist the urge to lie back across the bed and bring herself to a climax. She wanted to wait as long as possible before dulling the edge of her arousal.

"Thank you for this place, Robert," she said out loud. She hoped his spirit wasn't too shocked by her recent behavior. She didn't believe he could actually see her now, but she liked to think her feelings could somehow become the atmosphere around him if he chose to visit her in her dreams.

It began to rain, the sudden downpour drumming against the roof and on the boards of the porch nearly deafening her in all the right ways – every skeptical, supposedly realistic thought was drowned out, allowing her hopes and feelings to bloom passionately as she absorbed the unrestrained force beating down on the body of her house.

She cried out during a deafening boom that electrified all her primal nerve ends as she stepped instinctively away from the glass. She realized there was the very real danger of tornadoes, of a tree being struck and falling across her roof, but these possible threats couldn't ruin how thrilled she was by the atmosphere's power. The relentless pounding of the rain, the penetrating flashes of lightning and the groaning of thunder was all intensely sensual. She was about to retreat to the bed and bring herself to a climax when the silver pulses illuminating the darkness seemed to give sudden life to a tall, broad-shouldered silhouette standing out on her porch. She gasped, and then joyfully opened the door. The torrential downpour filled her room with a cresting wave of sound as John quickly stepped inside.

She slammed the door closed behind him, but not soon enough; the wind licked the front of her body with a cold wet tongue, making her shiver as her nipples turned to stone. He was soaking wet, yet his black hair looked almost the same slicked back against his skull, and water glistened in lovely glimmering droplets down his black leather jacket. She was the one who was trembling, her arms wrapped around herself as she watched him zip open his jacket and wrench it off impatiently. He slipped a hand beneath her hair, gripped her by the back of the neck, and pulled her to him.

All the sensual violence of the storm outside felt contained in his kiss as she was swept away on it, forced to submit to his determined exploration of her mouth as if the answer to every possible secret was buried in it. She wrapped her arms around his neck and clung to him, grateful for his warm strength against her chilled flesh. It seemed impossible that he was there and yet absolutely right as she wondered how she could possibly have gotten through the night if he hadn't arrived.

He moved his hand to her face and kept it turned up to his. "You were waiting for me," he observed, clutching one of her ass cheeks with his other hand and squeezing it painfully. "Did you miss me?"

"Yes, my lord!"

"You're a fascinating woman, Sofia."

"It wouldn't affect how I feel about you, I can't *help* how I feel about you, but I'm really hoping you're not married, John."

"Not anymore."

"Thank God!"

"Thank *me*. He joined us together, but I'm the one who separated us."

"Thank you, my lord. God, I can't imagine... I feel so sorry for her. How could she possibly stand to lose you?"

"She thought I was a sadistic bastard, that's how. But *you* don't seem to have a problem with that, do you?"

"No," she whispered, holding his eyes. She knew she didn't need to tell him he could do whatever he wanted to her.

He swept her up in his arms, carried her over to the bed, and spread her across it so her head and shoulders rested comfortably against a pillow. She gazed up at him almost worshipfully as he in turn regarded her sternly, his mouth hard and his eyes impenetrably dark in the dim light. He seated himself on the edge of the bed and she arched her back, straining for his kiss even as she kept her arms resting submissively at her sides, the way she had last night. Without taking his eyes off her face, he raised her head with one hand and with the other swept her hair above her head so it cascaded across the pillow. She knew the lamplight brought out the golden highlights in its light-brown depths; she could see how beautiful she was in his eyes as he stared down at her so seriously she suffered a stab of anxiety sharpened by excitement wondering what he had planned for her.

"Sofia," he whispered, brushing the ball of his left thumb across her brow, and then along the hollow of her cheekbone, as his right hand gently turned her face away, exposing the side of her neck still marred by the mysterious bite mark.

She held her breath, suddenly afraid. Her heart began beating faster, echoing the urgent pounding of the rain. She was looking in the direction of the French doors, and she saw lightning fork in luminous veins across the darkness as he bent towards her. He was the shadow cast by the bolt of electricity rising from the earth into the sky as pain flashed hot and blinding through her body. She cried out in fear because this wasn't a love bite by any stretch of the imagination; it truly felt like he was intent on sinking his teeth into her neck. She tried to push him away, but he caught her wrists and pinned them firmly over her head against the cool mantle of her hair.

"Oh, my God!" she gasped. "My God! My God!" She couldn't bear the threatening agony another second, she had to ask him what the hell he was doing, she had to beg him to stop, and yet she didn't, she couldn't, the sensation was so intense her body found it irresistible. She couldn't believe he was biting her neck like a vampire even as she seemed to feel her hot blood rushing from her pussy through her heart and willingly up into his mouth. He made a vicious, guttural sound deep in his own throat as she spread her legs and arched her back, her cunt aching to be penetrated with the same utterly unyielding strength, her misery intensified by how completely he ignored her writhing body. When he pulled back she went completely limp; he no longer needed to pin her wrists over her head for her to keep them there as he stared down at her.

"Have you always been this submissive?" he asked quietly.

"No, only with you, John," she whispered.

He waited.

"My lord!"

"They say it takes three bites, Sofia. Do you believe that?"

"I don't know… what happens after three bites?"

"You're mine forever."

"I already am," she dared to confess.

"And why do you think that is?" He gazed down the length of her body, running his hand lightly over her skin from between her breasts down to just above her sex, cruelly teasing her by resting it there, his fingers ignoring how deeply her pussy longed for them, for any hard and penetrating part of him.

"You read my dreams?" she asked helplessly.

"Yes. They would seem to explain some things."

She couldn't see any blood on his lips, but the side of her neck was throbbing and she couldn't be sure the hot wetness *wasn't* her blood...

"I feel like I've been waiting for you all my life, Sofia."

She moaned and clutched the pillow above her head, resisting the temptation to push his hand down between her legs. He was wearing a long-sleeved black shirt that intensified her longing to see his bare chest. "And I've been waiting for *you*!" she exclaimed breathlessly.

"And what have you been doing while you waited?" He kept his right hand resting firmly on her belly while he unbuckled his belt.

"Being with the wrong man."

"He never realized how kinky you are?"

"No, and if he had, he would have thought there was something wrong with me."

"Maybe there is." He stood up and whipped off his black leather belt, slipping it with practiced ease through the loops. "Maybe it's the same thing that's wrong with me because of what happened between us in a past life," he added. He dropped the belt on the bed beside her and unzipped his jeans.

"I don't know… I've always had vivid dreams, but not like those…"

"You need a safe word." He pulled off his shirt and flung it behind him. "I should have given you one the other night, but you didn't seem to want one."

"No…" She stared at his open fly, but he was wearing black underpants beneath his black jeans, so she fixed her eyes hungrily on his bare chest. His pecs were as firm as she had felt they were, and completely smooth. The only hair on him was a thin black line that stretched all the way from his heart down to his crotch, its flow broken by the tight little indentation of his navel. There was something feral about it that matched his goatee and made her pussy so wet she moaned in despair at his patience.

"So, what's it going to be, Sofia?" He reached down and yanked off one of his boots.

"I don't know… what do you mean?"

He removed his other boot. "Your safe word."

"Do I really need one?"

"Oh, yes." The ghost of a smile touched his lips that was truly sinister.

"*Cobzar*, that's a Romanian lute player."

"*Cobzar*… well, that's different. *Cobzar* it is." He pushed his jeans and underwear down and she got her first real look at his cock.

Even only partially erect, the dimensions of his penis were all she could have hoped for. Male striptease slang crossed her mind as she thought, *He's definitely a grower!* and she definitely preferred growers because you never knew how big and hard they could get; it all depended on how inspired they were… on how turned on she had the power to make him…

He stepped out of his jeans and discarded them as indifferently as he had the rest of his clothing. She bent her knees and spread her legs a little more, showing him the effect his naked body had on her even as she kept her arms raised submissively over her head. With Steve she had always been in control during sex, which had dulled the edge of her arousal even more than she realized. She was so aroused now that she felt profoundly languid. A man's legs usually disappointed her, they were either too stocky or too thin, but John's looked perfect to her, muscular and yet slender without being in the least bit scrawny. He was circumcised, and as his erection grew, responding to the appreciative caress of her eyes, she licked her lips, relishing how defined the head of his dick was, thick and distinct from the shaft, easily able to fill her throat and gag her…

He allowed her to look at him for a moment before he reached down and switched off the bedside lamp. The room was plunged into a darkness that made her feel more alive than ever as thunder rumbled and lightning flashed; she was intensely conscious of her own much smaller pulse so vulnerably wrapped in soft and easily penetrated flesh. She tensed beneath the sensation of his belt slithering across her belly like a snake, but she didn't have time to think about what it might mean before he slipped a hand beneath her back and pushed her over so she was lying face-down with her arms still raised over her head. She braced herself for the hot lick of leather, both desiring and dreading it, but it never came. Instead he caressed her hair out of the way, slipped the belt beneath her, and wrapped it around her neck. She moaned in trepidation, but also with relief that he wasn't doing anything so trite as beating her. The leather's inexorable pressure around her throat was much more thrilling precisely because it seriously worried her. She moaned expectantly as she felt him get on the bed with her.

"On your knees, Sofia."

She pushed herself up doggie style, or cat-like as she preferred to think of it. She kept her head up, forced to do so as he tugged on the belt, stretching it taut between them as he positioned himself behind her. The pressure around her throat was squeezing warm juices into her pussy as her body helplessly responded to the vital link between her breath and her sex which was all about life.

"Has any other man ever cut off your breath, Sofia?" He spoke sternly. "Did you ever ask any of your other lovers to do this to you?"

"No… my lord. It wasn't until I moved here that I started having fantasies about it for some reason, and then I had that dream…"

"And why do you think that is?"

"I don't know… please don't make me talk, my lord!"

"You hate that, don't you?"

She didn't respond as he rested his erection along the base of her spine, teasing her by making her feel how long it was and how deeply it could penetrate her, tormenting her pussy by ignoring it and threatening her with the possibility of a much more excruciating fulfillment should he decide to fuck her ass instead.

"You hate that so much because you don't want to think," he informed her almost tenderly, "because you think too much all the time."

"Yes..."

He reached down and pressed two fingertips against her clitoris. "You don't care about having an orgasm, do you?"

The answer was "No" and yet the way he began caressing her suddenly made her wonder if that was true as she whimpered in confusion.

He tugged on the belt, forcing her head back even more. There was something intensely arousing about the position... there could easily be another man kneeling on the bed in front of her getting ready to slip his big dick between her lips and all the way down her throat, which would caress him with even more dangerous fervor as John tightened his grip on the belt to assure her absolute submission to whatever they did to her. The mere thought stoked her excitement so much any discomfort felt irrelevant.

He dipped a finger into her pussy, pressing the base of his thumb against her clit. For some reason the slight pleasure annoyed her because it was so superficial; she was craving much more intense sensations than she could easily give herself. Suddenly she resented being told by feminists that the clitoris is the most important female sexual organ. That wasn't true, not for *her*. The deepest dimensions of her womb, the darkest recesses of her ass, and the vulnerable depths of her neck – having these roughly, violently, and even dangerously stroked turned her on like merely masturbating never could.

He withdrew his hand and inserted a finger slippery with her juices into her dry anus. Her tight little hole clenched instinctively around his digit as she moaned and made every conceivable helpless sound she could squeeze out of her constricted throat as he slowly penetrated her ass, his finger a harmless ambassador of the sensual battle to come when the determined force of his lust would defy all her physical limits. What really hurt was how much her pussy ached for his cock. Her cunt was as ready for him as her ass was not, and yet how tightly he had wrapped the belt around her throat mysteriously made her feel as if her neck was her most stimulatingly constricted orifice now. Her sphincter clenched around his finger when he pulled it out, making her conscious of the fact that she could also open herself up back there if she really wanted to. When he suddenly thrust his erection deep into her pussy the pleasure was shockingly absolute. She wondered how she could possibly use her safe word if she didn't have any breath with which to form it, but she wasn't at all afraid. His hard-on pulsed in and out of her in rhythm with lightning flashing outside, the silence in her head as he slowly cut off her breath filled by the roar of thunder like the memory of her freely flowing breath and blood. The more viciously he rammed the head of his cock against her cervix, the more it felt like the glowing horizon of her flesh in which her sensual soul was mysteriously concentrated and thriving on the rhythm of his intensifying pleasure, the pressure building in her chest a finite space in complete contrast to her sex, made so deep and wet by his violent thrusts that she felt bottomless. Thrust to the edge of physical existence, her body came stunningly alive and longed to remain there in this overwhelmingly fulfilling erotic fourth dimension forever.

* * *

The storm had passed and the rain gently drumming against the roof was soothing as a cat's purr. It was still dark in her bedroom where she lay in the crook of John's arm, her head resting on his chest, feeling she had always been there. The memory of lightning flashing and his dick pulsing inside her, his satisfied groans blending with rumbles of thunder, was vivid as a dream she had awoken from to the reality of his tenderness. She couldn't believe she had spent seven years lying in a similar position with another man every night. Her soul had known perfectly well she wasn't with her lord, but her personality had been foolishly afraid to be alone.

"What are you thinking, Sofia?"

"I'm thinking that I feel so comfortable with you."

His arm tightened around her as she caressed his chest, wondering at its firmness and strangeness, and yet at how mysteriously familiar it felt to the nerve ends in her fingertips.

"I'll come by tomorrow and build that coop for you," he said.

"You will?"

"I told you I would."

"Thank you, I would love that, mainly because it means I'll get to see you again tomorrow."

"You're going to be seeing a lot of me."

She smiled. "You make that sound like a threat."

"I'm merely warning you."

"You mean *promising* me. How could that be anything but a wonderful promise, my lord?"

"What if it gets to be too much for you, the things I enjoy doing to you, Sofia?"

"It would never be too much for me."

"How do you know?'

"I just do," she insisted fervently. "It could only be too little for me, never too much. I could only be disappointed if you weren't intense enough, if you were afraid to be as hard on me as I want you to be."

He reached up and caressed her face, brushing the hair away from her eyes so he could trace the line of her brow with his thumb. "Do you really believe I strangled you to death in a past life?"

"I don't know…"

"I didn't ask you if you knew, I asked you if you believed it."

"I don't know," she repeated lamely. "I think I do, *somehow*."

"But now that you're conscious of your violent fate in another incarnation, shouldn't that exorcise your demons?"

"You're assuming that my kinkiness is a result of trauma, but that's not all it's about."

"Go on," he urged, laying his hand over hers where it rested against his heart.

"I don't quite know how to express it except to say that somehow I feel so much more intensely beautiful and mysteriously invulnerable when… when you're using me like that."

"When, technically, you should feel just the opposite."

"It's strange, I know, but that's not how my soul responds to it."

"Your soul is very real to you, isn't it?"

"Yes, I suppose it is," she admitted, "even though I hadn't thought about it that way until lately."

"Until you moved here."

"Until I moved here," she echoed.

He brought her hand up to his mouth and kissed the heart of her palm "We still don't know anything about each other," he reminded her.

"Only some of the most important things."

"Do you think we'll ever be a dull, boring couple?"

"Never!" she replied fervently to cover up how happy the question made her.

"So there's nothing else you want to know about me?"

"Of course there is."

"Good, because I'm really looking forward to finding out everything about *you*, especially what you don't even know about yourself yet, Sofia, what you would never even dare imagine you could be like. I'm going to make you do things that right now would make you die of shame just to think about them, but you'll do them for *me*."

"Yes, my lord," she whispered, attempting to picture what dire ordeals he had planned for her, but she was so relaxed and content lying in his arms listening to the quiet drumming of the rain it was impossible. "I had no idea you raised cattle." She changed the subject.

"I don't."

"But I saw-"

"I rent part of my land out to a local farmer when he needs to rotate his herds."

"Oh… I asked the mail lady about you," she confessed.

"Did you?"

"Yes, that's why I was afraid you were still married."

"Anne and I separated six months ago, but she still gets mail here. I promised to hold it for her until she got back from Australia."

"Wow, what's she doing in Australia?"

"Getting as far away from me as possible, I suspect."

She laughed. "I find that very hard to believe."

"That's because you're as twisted as I am."

"I don't want to pry, John, but I'm curious to know…"

"What I do for a living?"

"Yes."

"In 1995 I started an ISP company."

"An Internet Service Provider?"

"Yes. It did pretty well."

"People dialing up your server to get on the Internet?"

"Exactly."

"How many people were subscribed to your ISP?"

"When I sold the company, approximately three-thousand five-hundred."

"Wow. That's a lot of people. Paying you *what*, ten dollars a month?"

"Thirteen. I sold the company, and now I raise chickens."

She laughed again. "What was the name of your company?"

"Does it matter?"

"I'm curious."

"Wolf.net."

"You *look* like a wolf."

"Do you realize how selfish that was of you to beg me to kill you, Sofia?" he said abruptly. "I loved you, we were engaged to be married, and yet you asked me to murder what I held most dear on earth."

"I'm sorry, my lord, but I wanted to die by your hand..."

"And you *keep* wanting to."

"Yes... but not really, you know, I don't actually *want* to-"

"No, you want to live on the edge. I'm so glad we found each other, Sofia. I hate to think what might have happened to you in the wrong hands." He caressed her hair and went on as if stroking the thoughts right out of her head. "You crave those transcendent moments when your flesh mysteriously fuses with the eternal energy inside you that created, and yet also somehow needs, the intoxicating warmth of your feeling and desires, which are so much more than you think, than we can ever really know, a divine force in and of themselves."

"*Oh, my lord!*" She buried her face in the side of his neck and wrapped her arms tightly around his chest, never intending to let him go.

Chapter Twelve

She had fallen asleep with her head pillowed against his chest, and when she woke up he was gone, only this time he had left her a note, *See you in the morning.* She pieced together his progress from her bed to her desk, where he found a blue post-it pad and a red pen and quickly wrote these five wonderful words before returning to her room and sticking the square fragment of paper on her nightstand. It amazed her that she had slept deeply enough not to notice when he removed his body from beneath hers. She usually woke up at the slightest provocation, which might explain why she remembered her dreams so vividly, but while he was still there, and after he left, she dreamed nothing at all.

Morning was the coldest time inside her house, where she rarely turned on the heat, disliking its artificial warmth and the way it dried out her skin. She quickly slipped into her black robe and slippers, opened the French doors, and stepped out onto her back porch. The crickets sounded louder and more electric than ever on this dreamy morning. A luminous mist cloaked John's field, reflecting the gentle sunlight without absorbing it. There wasn't a single cow to be seen, only this shining mist that also seemed to fall soothingly over her brain as she gazed out at it not thinking about anything. Her lungs inhaled the invigoratingly cold air, her flesh and feet snuggled contentedly in her robe and slippers, and that was all... but not quite, there was a serpent in paradise compelling her to bite into her contentment with jagged consonants and smooth vowels. She couldn't just stand out here and be mindlessly happy, she needed to try and capture in words the feelings inspired by this misty golden morning; to express how hauntingly beautiful it was...

She sighed and went back inside. Except for the note he had left her, there was no trace of John's presence in her home. He had put all his clothes back on and left, probably the way he had come. It was only eight o'clock, she suspected he wouldn't be by for a while, but she couldn't be sure, so she washed up and dressed, slipping into her favorite black cotton leggings and a blood-red sweatshirt. She couldn't very well dress up when he was coming over just to build a chicken coop. She would offer to help him, of course, and if there wasn't anything she could do, she would ply him with tea or coffee, and make him lunch, and give him whatever he wanted while he worked, including a blow job if he asked for it, or even if he didn't…

She entertained herself with similarly stimulating daydreams while she made herself breakfast, boiling one of the fresh eggs he had brought her to go with her whole wheat toast, all-fruit strawberry jam, and her decaff Green tea blended with chamomile. She ate at her desk, compelled to check her LSU e-mail account even though all her colleagues and former students knew she was on sabbatical and not to be disturbed. There were no important messages, and the minute she finished breakfast she turned off the computer, slipped on her jacket and stepped out onto her front porch. She brought a notepad and pen with her, and sitting in one of her fold-out blue chairs, she let the feelings that had been congealing inside her like that luminous mist take shape as solid words; the focused intensity of her mind trying to make sense of her sentimentally dense emotions.

The Atmosphere of Moments

Love can never express itself
fully enough embraced by time.
When you're young you think it's great
sex you want at one with true love.
Growing older it's a mysterious
merger of thoughts and earthly dreams

you need as the sun begins to rise
and set with alarming speed,
beating you with mortality
until you ache with compassion
for your self and all forms
of life, until you hope nothing –
all those lost persons and moments –
ever dies. Until you're forced to
have faith in the tree of your life
even though its roots are only theories
of darkness becoming matter through
light, and our thoughts are powerless
sentences silhouetted against the sky,
breathing this way of life into us by day,
exhaling boundless promises at night.

It seemed a strange poem to write after the intense sex she'd had lately, and yet it wasn't, because despite how little she still knew about John, she felt more comfortable, more mysteriously at peace with him than she had ever dreamed of feeling with Steve. She smiled remembering the much less poetic way he had expressed it last night, "Because you're as twisted as I am" yet his tone had been quietly serious, not at all flippant or sarcastic. If her dreams were more than just the manifestations of an overactive imagination, then he had kept his promise to find her again. The mere thought was hopelessly romantic, yet it felt entirely possible this morning with the trees as defined as her thoughts all framed by the luminous mist of her feelings. The sun would soon burn it away, and she was glad, because some things were just too intense to think about all day. There was no way to prove anything true, there was only how she felt, and this had to be evidence enough, somehow.

There were small wonders to be experienced all around her. For example, she realized two of the big bushes in her front yard, which had blossomed with leaves since she moved in, were Azaleas when she noticed purple buds sprouting everywhere. Spring was definitely on its way, heralded by the spider web she accidentally ran into as she walked around her house wondering what else she might discover. She made a mental note to order a botanical guide to the native trees and plants of Louisiana from amazon.com as soon as possible. It was sad how little she knew about nature's individual intricacies, especially now that she was surrounded by it. She discovered two other taller, narrower bushes that looked like little dead trees as a stray shaft of sunlight illuminated tiny buds glistening all over them. They were Hibiscus bushes – a humming bird tree. They looked so painfully dead from a distance that the miracle of life resurrecting every year struck her with fresh significance. Being depressed was like winter's seemingly lifeless branches which were actually still full of sap – of hope – and all it took was warmth from the right person to get it flowing, the penetrating understanding in his eyes stimulating her to grow inside and feel things she had never dared to believe before as she opened herself up to the stimulating force of his being...

Now that she was looking, Sofia realized many of the trees on her property were already sprouting light-green leaves in defiance of the cold and the number of dead branches she relished burning in the fire every night. She would need to make a trip to Home Depot in Zachary for some things, including humming bird feeders. She wondered if John was there now buying the materials for her chicken coop. The minutes were ticking by more slowly than seemed physically possible as she waited for him to show up. Centuries had passed faster than this single morning. One minute she was being strangled to death in a besieged castle, the next she was stretching her arms trustingly out of a crib, cooing with pleasure to find herself in a fresh body with budding senses, not caring that they dried up and died because they were always filled with the mysterious sap of memories transcending time...

It was impossible for her to take a pleasant walk out in nature without metaphysical thoughts spouting inside her and imbuing everything with an even more fascinating dimension than it already possessed on a physical level. She was a poet at heart, there was no denying it, and, it seemed, a budding mystic as well. She was shedding her agnostic classification like a shell that had never really fit her and relishing this new, intensely sensitive skin she was in whose defenses were courageously profound rather than comfortably superficial. She had made the decision to trust John before she knew him, and so far her intuition had not proved wrong. All her life surrounded by atheists, she had never been comfortable completely believing in things that lay outside the sphere of science, yet her dreams were leaving her no choice but to take the side of a part of her that could almost be termed psychic – someone marked by mysterious perceptions or understanding – even though there was nothing non-physical about the chemistry between her and John, it was very real indeed.

She heard gravel crunching beneath tires out on the "main" road and thought Kelly was making her run early today, but the sound didn't stop at her mailbox; it kept drawing closer. She hurried around the house and saw a white pick-up truck pulling up next to her car. She ran towards it as John leapt lithely out and walked around behind it.

"Good morning!" she called, tempted to add "my lord" but not quite able to get the words out in the casual light of day.

"Good morning, Sofia." He was already unloading the truck, beginning with a couple of two-by-fours he carried over to the edge of the trees a few yards to the west of her house. "I figure this is a good place for the coop," he said as she followed him. "It's convenient from the kitchen door, but not so close that their squawking will annoy you in the morning, unless you have the windows open, then there's no escaping it."

She wanted to say, "Don't I get a kiss good morning?" but his smile wiped this petulant disappointment clear out of her mind. She had never seen him smile like that, and for an instant she was blinded. Everything about him was so dark – his clothes, his hair, his goatee – that when he grinned it was like the sun suddenly showing up in the center of black clouds beaming the force of his soul straight into hers. Instead she asked, "Are chickens really that noisy all the time?"

"No, only in the morning after the sun rises and they can't understand while they're still cooped up." He paused beside her on his way back to the truck, adding quietly, "My girls are very vocal."

Lightning flashed in her womb, a hot, melting sensation. The way he said that sounded so sexy she didn't know how she could possibly survive jealously watching him use power towels and drive nails into wood all day long.

He pulled her to him, pressing her body firmly against his as he kissed her, tonguing her roughly, then lightly biting her bottom lip before pushing her away and holding her at arm's length. "Go make me some coffee," he commanded gently.

"Yes, my lord. Cream and sugar?"

"Please." He smiled again, and let go of her so she could obey him.

* * *

By mid-afternoon not only was the adorable little coop he had designed finished and ready to house up to five hens, he had also put chicken wire around it, extending the fence out towards the field so the girls had plenty of space in which to forage. He fashioned a gate Sofia could walk through, and provided her with bowls for water and food, as well as with one twenty-five pound bag of chicken food and another of hen scratch, plus a bushel of fresh hay for three nesting cubicles. He had even brought her three Rhode Island Reds from his own stock, two younger ones and a third seasoned layer he explained would act as the den mother. They had been pecking and scratching happily around the house all day, feasting on untold varieties of bugs while occasionally clucking excitedly. The adorable sounds they made delighted her, and she stood watching them for long stretches of time as they scratched and pecked, scratched and pecked, quickly scraping their splayed toes over the ground to reveal the dirt beneath, then staring straight ahead for a split second of intense anticipation before launching their beaks at the ground, where there always seemed to be something delectable for them to eat. When the coop was complete, John handed her a plastic cup half full of scratch and told her to round them up by laying a trail into the fenced in area. It worked like a charm, and he found a hose she hadn't even known was there curled up beneath a bush to fill their water bowl with. Then she closed the gate as he loaded his truck back up with the remains of two-by-fours, nails, and all his tools. She had only managed to get him to take one short break for lunch – hummus sandwiches with broccoli sprouts on whole-wheat bread, organic corn chips, gourmet pickles and bottled water. He declared everything delicious where they sat out on the front porch nourished by the temperate beauty of the day as much as anything, then he got right back to work. She discovered that when he began a project he liked to get it done, and she admired his strength and determination, not to mention his engineering abilities, even as she grew exhausted from lusting after him, especially when he pulled off his shirt and kept working in just his black jeans and boots. They didn't talk much at all. He was concentrating, and she was happy just to feast her eyes on him even though it was torture not being able to touch him.

It was four o'clock and the sun was already beginning to dip behind the trees when she realized he was getting ready to leave.

"Won't you stay for dinner, John, please?" she asked, desperate. Her pussy was so wet she felt she would die if he didn't soothe her ache with his hard cock... she longed for him to stroke her and build the entirely different physical creation of on orgasm using her body as he hammered his erection deep inside her...

He smiled as he opened the door to the truck. "I'd like to take all this stuff home to the shop and shower, but then I'll come back if you want me to."

"Of course I want you to. You could even shower here," she offered.

"I know I could." He got into the truck and closed the door. "But we'll save that pleasure for another day." He reached through the open window and pulled her face down to his by grabbing a fistful of her hair. He kissed her lips without opening his mouth. "Wear something sexy for me." He let go of her and started the engine.

"What time can I expect you?" She noticed it was becoming increasingly difficult to part from him.

"What time is it now?"

"Around four o'clock."

"I'll be back by seven. What are you planning to make for dinner? I'd like to bring the right wine to go with it."

"I was thinking of roast chicken with basmati rice." She glanced guiltily back at the coop.

"Sounds delicious. We'll have a quiet night, Sofia." He shifted gears. "No breath-play for you tonight, my lady. You need a little TLC for a change."

"I need both, my lord. It reminds me I'm more than just flesh."

His eyes narrowed as he regarded her darkly for a moment. "We'll continue this conversation later." He revved the engine, did a confident reverse U-turn, and drove off.

She stood rooted to the spot until she could no longer hear the sound of his tires crushing the gravel, then she went inside, quickly stripped off her clothes, spread herself back across the bed, and furiously rubbed her clit with three fingertips until she climaxed, almost instantly, the image of his rare and mysteriously feral smile branded into the darkness behind her closed eyelids.

Chapter Thirteen

Despite the fact that she would be carving a roasted bird and risked splattering herself with the juices, Sofia felt compelled to wear white. Perhaps subconsciously she desired to appear innocent on this, their third night together, in contrast to her previous incredibly slutty behavior. Or perhaps the need to wear white was not a trick of her self-esteem at all but a conscious choice with profound roots. As she slipped into the sleeveless, low-cut tunic, she sensually reinforced the truth that she didn't feel guilty about the kinky darkness she had recently unearthed in her nature. There was something mysteriously pure about such intensity of emotion and sensation that inspired a reverent attitude towards the unplumbed depths of her sexuality. She had bought this dress because, like its black counterpart, it was timeless, its simple, gently form-fitting cut evocative of countless cultures and civilizations. It evoked ancient Egypt, a Greek *chiton*, the white shift of the Catholic novitiate, the undergarment of a Medieval princess, the nightgown of a 19th century governess... she was countless women in it, and yet how beautiful she looked was unique.

She rifled through the wooden boxes in which she kept her jewelry, mostly costume pieces she rarely wore but couldn't bring herself to throw out. Such a plain dress, and backless white high-heeled leather sandals, called for something colorful or extravagant to contrast with its classic lines. She had completely forgotten about the silver Gothic-style cross she had bought on impulse one day in a New Orlean's thrift shop. It was completely over the top, elaborately forged by flowering vines that imbued the Christian symbol with a pagan aura, and it hung from a thin white leather cord. She slipped it on and was pleased by the way it rested in her cleavage. It wasn't shaped like the cross on which Christ was crucified because all four parts met in the center like the petals of a flower, which its shape resembled. For some reason she really wanted to wear it tonight even though no other jewelry she owned would work with it. She opened a drawer, as a final touch intending to find a pair of white thong panties to slip on beneath her dress, but then suddenly thought better of it. She wasn't bleeding; she didn't need any panties. She wanted her pussy exposed to the atmosphere, and to his fingers and his cock and his tongue, to anything he might feel like thrusting inside her.

One reason she had decided on chicken for tonight was because she could prepare dinner in advance and be free to relax and enjoy his company, which she knew would make it hard for her to concentrate on any complicated recipe. The bird was in the oven roasting, and the basmati rice was cooking at very low heat over which it could sit for hours if need be. She had also tossed together a salad of Romaine lettuce, spinach, parsley, chopped walnuts and extra sharp cheddar cheese to serve with a vinaigrette. This simple meal was one of her favorites, but it was the company she was looking forward to more than anything.

She set the large table in the dining room with burgundy cloth placemats, violet cloth napkins, her good silverware, and the two red wine glasses she used only on special occasions. Two white wine glasses were already chilling in the refrigerator. The large space – empty except for a small pile of boxes she hadn't yet unpacked – echoed cavernously as she moved across the wooden floor in her high-heels. It seemed strange to be eating in a room that didn't even appear lived in, but the formal setting symbolized how serious she felt about this man. The room with the fireplace was all hers for the present, but this part of the house represented the future, and it meant a lot to her that already she had miraculously met someone who – she fervently hoped – could help her bring it to life.

The clock on the stove was glowing 7:00 in green numbers when she heard the unmistakable sound of a vehicle approaching along the gravel road. All her windows were open to the evening breeze and the distant sound wafted clearly towards her between the trees. She went and stood out on the porch to wait for him, and the vision of his white truck was the most beautiful thing she could imagine lighting up the dusk. A line from one of her favorite old songs wafted through her mind, *Nights in white satin, never reaching the end…* Not even a unicorn could have looked more wonderful than that plain white truck magically pulling into her driveway. How on earth had she managed to meet him? It didn't seem possible that he was real and not just a daydream walking towards her holding a bottle of wine. Over the black jeans and boots he seemed to live in he was wearing a white, long-sleeved button down shirt that also seemed to glow in the shadowy twilight beneath her trees. She remembered the way he had stripped out of his clothes last night and wondered if maybe she shouldn't have worn panties after all, because already her pussy was wet after only seconds in his presence

"Good evening, Sofia."

"Good evening." She accepted the bottle of wine even though she would have preferred to take *him* in her arms. "Thank you."

"You look beautiful." He immediately noticed the cross she was wearing and rested it in his hand as he studied it. "This isn't a Catholic cross," he observed with a note of relief in his voice.

"No, it's not. I bought it in New Orleans about a year ago. It's a little over the top, I know, but it spoke to me."

"It looks striking on you." He rested it between her breasts again, letting his fingertips lightly caress her skin. "Anything would."

"Thank you." Smiling happily, she opened the door and preceded him into the house, setting the wine bottle down on the table.

"Very nice," he said quietly, "and thank you for not putting us at opposite ends."

"Of course not!" She laughed. "I want to be close to you."

"I'm glad. If we're going to play lord and lady of the castle, I'd rather do it in bed."

"This table was here when I moved in." She walked into the kitchen. "Would you like a glass of white wine to start?"

He followed her. "I'd love one."

She opened the refrigerator and pulled out the bottle of *Toasted Head*, one of her favorite California Chardonnays.

He took it from her, and opened it with the corkscrew already resting on the counter as she got out the two chilled glasses.

"You think of everything," he observed approvingly.

"I chill my glass every night."

He smiled as he poured the wine for them. "You mean I'm not getting any special treatment?"

"Of course you are... I mean..."

"Relax, I'm only teasing you."

"I'm sorry, I just don't know how to react when a *dream* teases me!"

"What do you mean?" He touched his glass to hers, encouraging her to drink before she replied.

"I don't know... I just didn't expect..."

"To meet someone again so soon?"

"Yes, but you're not just *someone*..."

"Neither are you, Sofia."

"First I dreamed about you, and then you were just sitting on my porch when I got home... things like that just don't happen!"

"Obviously, they do." He sipped his wine and stared out the window behind her. "I've always believed I have the power to create my own destiny, but relationships complicate things, tie up your energies, and before you know it years have passed and you suddenly realize you aren't the person you thought you were."

She knew he was referring to his ex-wife because it was just how she felt about Steve. "With me it was because I was too afraid to let go and be alone again," she said.

"That's part of it," he agreed, still looking past her. "You can't blame the other person, at least not for everything. Fear of loneliness is just one of many fears that can eat away at our soul like termites until one day everything just collapses. You're lucky if it happens sooner than later and you have a chance to live your life the way you really want to. You can see clearly all of a sudden; all the walls you built up around yourself, for whatever reason, aren't there anymore, at least for a while."

"Yes, exactly! But nothing we do is a waste; I can't believe that. Something must have been happening inside us that got us to this point even while we *seemed* to be wasting our time..."

He took another swig of wine and brought his gaze back inside the house and into her eyes. "We were going through the dark time in our life, Sofia, the time of initiation when we were forced to confront all our fears and doubts precisely because we tried to run away from them."

"We were plunged into the darkness of despair in order to find the light inside ourselves?"

He smiled. "You're a Gnostic, my lady."

"As in the lost gospels?"

"No, in that sense 'Gnostic' means 'false', as in the 'false gospels', however, Gnosis is what those gospels preach – a way of knowing that brings the initiate into intimate touch with divine reality. It can't be taught, only achieved through initiation, as opposed to traditional Christianity, and the Holy Roman Catholic church specifically, which forces you to accept a body of dogma so that, hopefully, your sins will be forgiven and you'll achieve a rather boring eternal life. Traditional Christianity embraces blind faith and sexual guilt vs. the Gnostic path of empowered feelings and personal, including sensual, knowledge." He cradled her cross in his free hand and pondered it for a moment before concluding, very quietly, "We've definitely met before, Sofia."

"In my darkest hour, when I lost both my best friend, a man I truly loved, and the man I thought I loved, I remembered you, my lord. That's when I had the first dream…"

"For six months I waited here!" He gripped the cross passionately, staring into her eyes. "I wondered why I didn't leave, Sofia, why I didn't just sell the land and take off to Europe for a year or two, see more of the world, maybe visit India or Japan, or both. Anne and I lived here for five years, the memory of her poisoned every goddamn leaf and blade of grass, yet I endured it because, for some reason, I couldn't leave. Her ghost faded sooner than I thought it would, and then I was glad I'd stayed, but I was still making plans to go away, to lock up the house and take off for a long time, when at last you showed up. You almost made me wait too long, my love. God knows when I would have come back, if ever, and by then you might not have been living here anymore, and even if you were, you'd probably be with the wrong man again. A beautiful woman like you can't be alone for long." He let go of the cross. "You shouldn't be."

"No, John, I wouldn't have been with another man, I would have been dreaming of you and waiting for you, I know I would have, but I'm so glad I didn't have to! I'm so glad you stayed!" He had called her *my love* but she couldn't think about that yet, if she did her knees might give way and the chicken would burn and she wouldn't be able to concentrate on serving it, or on anything else.

He picked up the wine bottle, and topped off both their glasses. "Do we have time to sit out on the porch and talk for a while before dinner?"

"Of course."

"Good, because I know more about your past life than I do about this one."

* * *

Sofia hadn't talked so much since before Robert died, only with this man she didn't have to hold any of herself back, she felt she could – and she did – tell him everything she could think of. They talked out on the porch until the expensive organic bird in the oven was in danger of burning, then they came back inside and continued conversing by candlelight as they dined. Even if he had left right after dinner, it would still have been the perfect evening, but it didn't end there. He told her to get a flashlight and slip on some comfortable shoes, and together they walked out to the chicken coop. The hens were already inside; all she had to do was close the wire-mesh door and lock it with the metal clasp he had made raccoon-proof. Her favorite part of the coop was the back, where there were three little panels that lifted up so she could reach inside and grab the freshly laid eggs. With their large, brilliant orange yokes, the eggs he had given her tasted far better than the organic eggs she bought at *Whole Foods*. She was falling in love with the man standing beside her in the dark and with everything; she couldn't tell the difference. She didn't want to admit it, but he was right, she couldn't have endured living out here all alone, not for long, and just thinking about what might have happened filled her with despair. She remembered how during their first meeting he had warned her there were a lot of predators out here, yet that was how she felt about the city, where she had lived in apartments like chicken coops surrounded by emotional, physical and spiritual perils she was only now becoming fully aware of. Out here she was free to be herself like never before as she truly began plumbing the depths of who she was, and the deeper she looked inside herself, the more mystery she saw and the older she felt in an invigorating sense that made her feel timelessly young.

He switched off the flashlight and they walked back to the house in the dark, guided by the glimmer of candles still burning on the dining room table more faintly than the stars sparkling overhead in the clear black sky.

"You need some furniture," he had observed at dinner. "I'd be happy to build you some."

She had discovered that her lover was a capitalist, a farmer and a craftsman, and since apparently he was wealthy enough to travel the world for a few years at will, she added investment banker to the list. That he was also the most sexually exciting man she had ever met was part of the whole mysteriously fascinating equation of who he was.

"That's a Templar cross you're wearing around your neck," he remarked as he filled her glass with the wonderful red wine he had brought.

She had replied without a second thought, "You were once a Templar, my lord, a *true* knight of God."

"You think so?"

She was beginning to recognize the cool tone of voice with which he greeted her most intense remarks – it meant he was more pleased by her comment than he cared to admit.

They talked briefly about where they grew up and where they went to school, about her career and his former entrepreneurship, about their favorite music and movies and foods, but they avoided discussing any details about their respective "dark" years, which had culminated in this emotionally luminous evening that made her feel her life had only just begun.

As they walked back into the house, the open space echoing the sound of his boots, he asked, "Are you going to let me build you some furniture, Sofia?"

"Of course, I would be honored! It just seems like so much trouble…"

"Nothing is too much trouble for you." He went into the kitchen to put the flashlight back in the laundry room, and while he was gone she slipped back into her high-heels. "Besides, it's not trouble, it's pleasure," he said firmly when he returned. "I love working with my hands." He reached down and pulled her dress off, leaving her no choice but to raise her arms over her head and assist him in stripping her. He stood gazing at her naked body by the flickering candlelight, walking slowly around her holding her dress in both his hands, and for some reason she thought of a priest performing a sacrament.

"Your body belongs to me as much as to you now, Sofia."

"Yes, my lord."

He draped the dress over a chair and picked up one of the candles burning in an antique brass pillar. "Come here." He took her hand and led her into the bedroom. Her heels ticked like a clock even as she was possessed by a sense of timelessness.

He set the candle down on the nightstand, and surprised her by perching on the edge of the bed to pull off his boots before he spread himself back across it.

"Come here," he said again, and she happily slipped out of her shoes to lie beside him, cradling her head against his chest and slipping her hand into his shirt. The top three buttons were undone, but she couldn't caress enough of his chest to satisfy her, and she moaned in frustration.

"Did you masturbate after I left this afternoon, Sofia?"

The question shocked her, and then she wondered why. "Yes, my lord…"

"You've wanted my cock all day, haven't you?"

"Yes..."

He unbuckled his belt and unzipped his jeans. "Suck it." He shoved his underwear down and wrested his hard-on out straight up into her mouth because she was already crouching hungrily over him.

He tasted like the wine she had drunk and warm flesh and smelled of earth and soap, and something else indefinably irresistible. His skin was smooth and silky, and she relished the slick, ravenous sounds she made sucking him down, bracing herself on his hard thighs as she took all of him into her mouth; ringing the full length of his erection with her lips while swirling her tongue around it, submerging him in a whirlpool of firm, soft and hot sensations even as she moved a hand down to cradle his cool and tender balls, clutching them gently but possessively. She wasn't satisfied until he groaned, almost inaudibly, but the quiet sound reverberated triumphantly through her soul and inspired her to give him the blowjob of his life. When he abruptly grabbed her head with both hands, she moaned too, in gratitude that he was using her orifice they way she longed for him to, completely, not just concentrating on her devoted lips and energetic tongue but savoring her vulnerable throat, too. He caressed as much of his dick as he could with the inside of her neck, moving her face swiftly up and down over him. He threaded his fingers through her hair to get a better grip on her head, and she concentrated on breathing through her nose as he used her selfishly, never even giving her a chance to swallow the semen collecting in the hollow of her throat and threatening to gag her in combination with his thrusts.

She was increasingly uncomfortable, and utterly content.

He skull-fucked her for such a long time she was surprised and disappointed when he didn't come in her mouth in the end. He pulled out and commanded her silently, with his hands gripping her arms, to sit on his cock. She straddled him breathlessly, bracing herself on his chest with one hand while with the other she stroked her clitoris, afraid she couldn't take how big and hard he was so swiftly. He gave her just a few seconds before he gripped her hips and slid her cunt down around him. She cried out as he forced his erection past her dry opening into the slick, warm depths that embraced him with intense relief that he was finally filling up the smoldering wet emptiness she had suffered all day.

"Touch yourself the way you did this afternoon, Sofia. I want to see you come. And don't close your eyes. You're going to watch me watching you."

She moaned and obeyed him, of course, it was the easiest thing in the world to do, and the hardest, too, because even by the soft glow of candle-light she felt shy wondering if her face would be contorted by ecstasy or somehow become lovelier than ever.

He reached up and rubbed her nipples between his thumb and fore-finger, squeezing and rubbing in rhythm with her wrists working between her legs. She didn't slide her pussy up and down his cock; she kept it planted as deep inside her as possible, the open folds of his jeans tormenting her because they prevented her from getting absolutely all of him inside her.

"I said look at me," he commanded when she forgot and closed her eyes to follow the luminous path of the climax igniting in her pelvis and swiftly escalating towards an implosion of pure pleasure her flesh would somehow contain and survive.

She opened her eyes again and somehow kept them open staring down into his even as the orgasm she gave herself impaled on his erection literally blew her mind. She didn't care at all what she looked or sounded like as he lifted his hips off the bed and rammed his pulsing dick in and out of her pussy as he came with her.

Chapter Fourteen

She was in an empty church. It was the dead of night. She had rested her head on the pillow and closed her eyes, then a second later she opened them again and was there. It wasn't a normal dream because she knew where her body was – lying in bed in another dimension that wasn't as real as this one. At first all she could feel was relief to finally be here. Then she was consumed by sadness at how long it had taken her awareness to shift the vital degree needed to put the reality that always existed just outside her flesh into focus, so she could truly see it and experience it. She had been in this particular place before, of that she was certain even though a long time had passed since her soul commanded a mind with the knowledge to realize it. Relief and regret gave way to an excitement tempered by uncertainty, because she didn't quite know what she was doing here now. She felt she *should* know, that it was imperative she remember, but the truth was buried too deep inside her.

Sofia looked around her, amazed by the clarity of the details her dreaming eyes could perceive and focus on for more than a blurry second. She had to write all this down when she woke up so she wouldn't forget anything, and she looked forward to telling John about the intricately carved columns. It was dark in the church, but not cold; the atmosphere vibrated on the same frequency as her feelings. She searched for the source of the faint illumination that just barely enabled her to make out the carvings, but she couldn't find it. The golden glow was subtle as candlelight, yet it didn't flicker, or appear to rely on any substance to sustain it. The soft light created hosts of shadows and seemed to be coming from the center of the chapel. She walked towards it past rows of empty pews even though she would have liked to linger over the columns with their beautiful bas-reliefs depicting all the bounties of nature – flowering trees and bushes and vines, cows and horses, fish and fowl – pagan iconography in a Christian building. The altar dedicated to Christ's mass was covered by a white cloth that literally glowed in the dark, but that wasn't surprising because she knew that fabric, like everything else, is only an illusion; all matter is truly energy mysteriously given form by consciousness. When she saw the opening in the stone floor, she was gripped by an excitement so intense it was purely sexual. The light had seemed to be rising out of it, but now she thought it must be emanating from the stone beneath her feet because the wound in the earth before her was pitch-black. The longer she stared down at it the hotter she got and the less she could feel the difference between this hole in the ground and the one between her legs. To be frightened of it would be as foolish as fearing her own sex. Even though she couldn't see them, she knew there were steps leading down deep into the ground and she gladly followed them, her bare feet easily finding the stairs plunging into the earth. Only then did she become aware of the plain white shift she was wearing, sleeveless and low-cut, that fell to her ankles.

Lights flickered in the distance beneath her as if the star-filled sky was below her, otherwise she could see absolutely nothing. The darkness was impenetrable and the farther she descended the more aroused she became, as though she was actually ascending inside. To say that she was turned was like comparing a candle to the sun. There was no earthly way to satisfy her, yet she knew that whatever happened to her would feel impossibly good. Her lord was waiting for her, she could suddenly feel his presence. Without him she was lost, she was nothing…

When she touched bottom she suddenly saw on either side of her the carved effigies of two knights resting on the stone floor, their gloved hands gripping the hilts of swords stretching the length of their armored bodies. There was an explosion of heat in her chest she recognized as grief when she saw the profile of the man buried on her left, and the sensation of sadness and loss was so intense she began waking up…

"Sofia."

The sound of her name divided her in half because she couldn't tell if it was coming from her bedroom in the woods or from the crypt below the heart of a church. Then she understood there was no real difference between them, and the dream solidified around her again as John stepped towards her out of the darkness. She was so happy to see him she wondered shy she didn't run straight into his arms, but part of her knew why, and was thrilled beyond measure. He was dressed entirely in black, all she could see of him was his face, and suddenly she caught the scent of leather all around her, an invigorating, living smell. It was as if this bowel in the earth was home to all the reptiles from which the tough skins had come to protect the more sensitive flesh of the men she glimpsed standing in the shadows around her, watching intently as John gripped her wrists in his gloved hands and raised her arms straight up over her head. Again she was afraid she would wake up as she felt herself being suspended, her feet rising off the floor so her toes pointed down like a dancer's barely grazing the stone, and she was possessed by an almost unbearably beautiful feeling of grace beating at the haunting heart of her helplessness. The only thing she couldn't tolerate anymore was the dress she was wearing. She was desperate for him to rip it off like a shroud and reveal the hot galaxies of her aureoles sprouting lusciously firm nipples. Her flesh responded to the sight of the dagger in his hand with a flash of lust that nearly caused her to black out it was so sharp and cut her so deep. The pleasure was nearly intolerable as he clutched the dress over her heart and cut the it off her slowly, staring into her eyes as he licked her flesh with the tip of the blade. The fiery caress felt like a blessing to her smoldering sex, the countless veins and capillaries branching through her body transformed into a burning bush of unquenchable desire.

At last she was naked, and she understood then where the soft light had been coming from all along, not from the stones, not from the hole in the ground, not from hidden candles, but from her own skin. Her flesh was the luminous warmth revealing the earthen walls of the crypt. There was no God she could pray to for relief from the longing to be absolutely controlled and violently used, there was only her lord before her, he was everything and she was all his, she had come from him, she would come for him, there was no difference. Endless thrusts of unmitigated force would never be enough to satisfy her, but it was all she longed for forever....

He sheathed the knife in a leather scabbard hanging from his hips, from which he then unwound a long black whip. He turned his back on her as if to walk away, but then abruptly faced her again and the agonizingly fine leather sliced across her breasts, the snake-like tip giving one of her nipples a flaming kiss. The pain was so intense she nearly climaxed, and the only thing she dreaded was waking up.

"Oh, my lord!" she sighed. "I love you more than anything!"

"I *am* everything," he sliced the whip across her womb, "through you, Sofia."

The agony blazed through her like an orgasm, her innermost muscles clenching and shuddering with joy. Two more men stepped out of the darkness, both of them holding whips in their black-gloved hands, and she was filled with despair knowing she couldn't remain suspended between dimensions much longer. A steam-like hiss issued from the crypt as three whips all snaked across her body at the same time, one licking her breasts, the other the infinitely sensitive flesh just above her sex, and the third the breathtakingly tender skin of her thighs. It was too much for her... she woke up in the throes of a climax, her hand working between her thighs, and a moan of superficial fulfillment mingled with profound disappointment rose from her throat where she lay in bed alone.

* * *

Although part of her had obviously been into it, Sofia didn't quite know what to make of her latest dream. It definitely fell into the category of "fantasy" because she knew for a fact she would not enjoy being whipped in real life. Or would she? Answers to questions she once took for granted weren't quite as obvious to her now that her reaction to things wasn't constricted by Steve's appallingly conventional mind-set. How could she not have realized when she was living with him how typically superficial and profoundly boring he was? In retrospect it seemed obvious it was Robert she had really been in love with and Steve had served as her fuck-puppet, her living sex toy, the cute male pet she fed and cuddled with every night in front of the television set. It wasn't the fact that he was five years younger that had made him so wrong for her. She was increasingly ashamed of the person she had been when they were together. In many ways she had used him, convincing herself she was in love with him to romanticize a base need for companionship and sex. She had allowed her body's needs to rule the desires of her soul for so long that a violent end was inevitable. She didn't feel any guilt – in his own way Steve had used her as much as she had used him – but she did feel ashamed of herself. It must have pained Robert to no end to see her wasting herself like that.

She was going to John's house tonight. She was so excited and nervous at the same time that the two feelings mysteriously cancelled each other out and left her helplessly in the thrall of that vivid and sinister dream. It still felt much more real than her waking life as she cleaned the kitchen and the bathroom, and then dumped the ashes from the fireplace around the roots of the budding Hibiscus bushes. Letting the chickens out of their coop, and tossing generous handfuls of scratch to them, had provided a soothing interlude earlier that morning, during which she thought of nothing at all as she watched them. Their clucking energy was hypnotically soothing, and during the day she kept going out to see them and feed them. When later in the afternoon she checked for eggs, she couldn't believe it when she saw one lying in a hollow in the straw, smooth and perfect, light-brown and still warm to the touch. She grasped it gently in her hand and carried it into the house, filled with awe. It was much bigger than the organic eggs from *Whole Foods* it was temporarily sharing a carton with. It seemed a dream never having to buy eggs again, but then again everything was a dream living out here, an intensely sensual and demandingly real dream...

It took her hours to get ready. First she took a long bath, during which she shaved her legs and then her pussy so it was smooth as alabaster to the touch and as soft as flesh could be. She caressed a delicately scented moisturizing lotion all over her body, and blow-dried her hair, something she rarely did. She was still naked as she put on her make-up, taking great pains to make it seem as if she wasn't wearing any at all. Finally she slipped into the black counterpart of the white dress she had worn last night, once again forgoing a bra and panties. Black strap high-heeled sandals and the cross he had admired were all the accessories she needed besides a small black purse. She was driving to his house.

The hens had already tucked themselves in for the night when she went to lock them up. She had to keep their water bowl filled, and it would be necessary to clean out their coop every week, but she was surprised and pleased by how fun and easy they were to take care of, and by how generously she was rewarded for her minimal efforts, because a delicious egg was one of life's small but priceless pleasures.

"Good night, sweeties," she said, her voice high with excitement as she wondered what John's home was like. His wife had been gone for six months, she was confident he had taken complete possession of the place again, at least she hoped so because she wasn't looking forward to seeing traces of another woman. But that wasn't what was making her so nervous...

She left the porch lights burning as she got in the car and started down the gravel drive. The dusk was soft and deep; it had been another lovely sunny day. His house was on the other side of the field from hers, too far to walk in high-heels, but a quick and easy drive, during which all she saw were grazing horses and plump white sheep. It was surprising how luminous the sky was out here, as if there were still hours left in the day, whereas deep in her little forest night had nearly fallen.

"Oh, my God! That *can't* be it!"

There wasn't another house for miles, this *had* to be it, but she drove down the long driveway as slowly as possible, giving herself time to believe it. Her lover lived in a white mansion that would have been right at home on a plantation, although thankfully the faux Greek columns were missing. The two sides of the house she could see were surrounded by a screened-in porch with a stunning view of a small lake surrounded by gently undulating land ringed with trees. His rustic welcome basket, his casual uniform of black jeans and boots, his white pick-up-truck, two-by-fours and chicken coops, had not prepared her for *this*.

She followed the packed dirt driveway (there was no noisy gravel here) to the front of the house, worried again this might not be the right place because his truck was nowhere in sight. She told herself it was probably parked in back as she got out and stood savoring the cool twilight breeze for a bracing moment. The silence was so absolute she could almost hear her heart beating as she started carefully up the front steps. It was too dark inside the screened in porch on either side of the main entrance to see anything, but she vaguely distinguished tall potted plants and plush, comfortable-looking wicker furniture flanked by tables and every other possible comfort. The double front doors were painted black and were so imposing she almost laughed. Fortunately there was a doorbell; her knuckles wouldn't have been able to rap loudly enough to be heard any farther than a few feet.

She rang the bell and stood literally holding her breath for a moment before she forced herself to exhale slowly; calmly. She told herself again what she had been trying to convince herself of all day – that she wasn't any-more vulnerable here than she was at home. When he cut off her breath in her own bed it was just as dangerous as doing it anywhere else, there was no reason for her to be nervous about being on his turf… in his lair…

* * *

"Where's your garden, John? I didn't see it as I was driving up."

"It's out back. You can't see everything from the main road, Sofia."

"No, I suppose not." They were sitting in one corner of the endless screened in porch. The cushions covering the white wicker furniture were amazingly comfortable, and she was still reeling from her brief view of the inside of the house. A grand staircase worthy of Scarlet herself ascended to a horseshoe-shaped open hallway overlooking the first floor, large enough to serve as a ballroom, with individual rooms opening off it, including the kitchen he immediately led her into that was nearly as big as her house, and which obviously served as an informal living room and dining room as well.

"I basically live in here," he had told her, which she could well believe because the rest of the house echoed like a museum as she walked across the polished wooden floor in her high-heels.

"You must have a cleaning lady," she remarked now as they relaxed out on the porch with some Chardonnay; she was drinking hers a little too quickly.

"Rosy. She comes in twice a week."

"Does she leave you gourmet meals in the fridge, too?" she asked cattily.

He smiled. "If she left me anything it would probably be fried pizza, boiled crayfish or Gumbo. I prefer to cook for myself."

"You do? Wow."

"You're wondering why on earth I live in such a big house, aren't you?"

"Well, yes... but maybe you and your wife planned on having lots of kids?"

"No."

His firm, monosyllabic answer discouraged her from pursuing the subject. Night took much longer to fall here than it did on her porch in the forest. She fixed her gaze on a pair of irises rising from a black vase beside her, her vision soothed and enchanted by the way the violet petals deepened as the air darkened, revealing the lovely color's inwardly luminous frequency.

"Anne wanted this house more than anything," he spoke suddenly, "and more than anything I wanted to please her. I knew it was too big, but it's what she wanted, and that's all that mattered."

"It must have cost a fortune."

"That's the thing, it didn't. The owner needed to sell, and this is East Feliciana Parish. Property taxes are almost non-existent."

"Well, *that's* good to know!"

"I estimate you'll pay around three-hundred dollars a year for your place."

"Are you kidding?" She was astounded, and relieved. "That's great!"

"Most of the furniture was hers. That's why some of the rooms look a lit-tle empty. She put it all in storage before she went away."

"Mm."

"I'll pour us another glass of wine and give you a tour."

"Okay."

The rooms opening off the main floor were all different, and each one was cozy in its own way despite the marked absence of furniture, but she especial-ly liked his study. Everything in here had obviously always been his, including all the books filling the floor-to-ceiling shelves, and the old-fashioned mahogany desk set in front of a window. There was also a stone fireplace twice the size of hers, and a black leather couch big enough to sleep on quite com-fortably. She didn't notice a narrow wooden door hidden in a corner of the room until he walked towards it, slipped a key out of his jeans, and unlocked it.

"Put your glass down, Sofia."

She obeyed him instantly, glad of the coaster on the polished table she was standing next to.

"I'm going to show you one of the reasons Anne and I split up. It wasn't the only reason, but it certainly wasn't the least important. You could say it was a symbol of the vital, irreconcilable differences between us."

If she was a cat she would have died in that moment she was so curious.

"After you, my lady." He held the door open for her.

She walked past him, then paused on the landing of an almost impassably narrow, low-ceilinged staircase that twisted downwards.

"Until I bought the house, this merely led to the root cellar. Go on, Sofia, don't be afraid."

"Should I be?"

"That all depends."

She didn't move even though her dream was pulling on her blood, urging her to walk down the steps. "On what?" she asked softly.

"On what you really want," he replied just as quietly.

"What if I'm not sure what I really want, John?"

"I know what you want, Sofia. Trust me."

Maybe she was easy, but that was all she needed to hear. She started down the steps, planting her hands on the confining walls because her high-heels made the steep descent treacherous. He hadn't suggested she remove her shoes, he was enjoying her helplessness, and she respected this about him much more than she resented it.

"How old *is* this house?" she asked, disturbed by how strangely unnatural her voice sounded in the confines of a stairwell which had clearly not been built for a modern physique.

"Old enough."

She didn't need to be told only slaves and servants had used this stairwell, she could feel it, and suddenly she was genuinely frightened. The steps were so worn she could easily break her neck if she wasn't careful. Yet he was right behind her, she was confident he would catch her if she stumbled. The light behind them was as good as useless once she made the first turn, at which point she was grateful to realize there was another dim light burning down in the cellar.

It didn't feel anything like her dream when she stepped onto the concrete floor; all she experienced was relief that she had made it down in one piece. The dim bulb hanging directly above her served to cast more shadows than light, so that at first she didn't quite understand what she was seeing around her.

He pressed his body up against hers from behind and caressed her dress up her thighs with both hands.

"My God!" she breathed. "Is this where the plantation owner punished and tortured his slaves when they misbehaved?"

"No, Sofia," he whispered into her hair, "this is where a beautiful woman like you gets disciplined."

"You mean all those... all those *things* aren't antiques?"

"Hardly. I made them all myself quite recently."

She remembered his skill with two-by-fours, and experienced a pang of sympathy for his wife. "When you got married, did Anne know what... what you like?" she dared to ask.

"I never went so far with her, because she never inspired me to. She thought I was furnishing this space as part of a plan to set up some kinky internet photo site and make even more money than I already had exploiting the web. She even offered to help find me some pretty models, and I let her go on thinking that because I wasn't entirely sure myself why I was building all this stuff. When she realized I wanted *her* to help me play with my new toys... well, that's when all the problems we'd been having came to a head."

"Like a dormant volcano suddenly erupting, I know. I've been there. You can only suppress your real self for so long before all the forces mysteriously working inside you demand an outlet. It's like-"

"I love you, Sofia."

"I love you too, John!" It was an immense relief to finally be able to say it.

"Raise your arms."

She hesitated an instant before obeying him.

"Anne knew I liked it rough." He pulled her dress off over her head. "But it wasn't until I had the time, and this place, that I began to truly explore my proclivities."

"I see…" The same thing had essentially happened to her, and here they were, together in the heavenly hell of all her darkest fantasies about to be realized.

He reached around and clutched her breasts, his firm, tanned hands a striking contrast to her soft, pale skin as she looked down at them, biting her lip anxiously. "You have the most incredible nipples I have ever seen, Sofia." He trapped them between his thumb and forefinger.

She cried out in pain as he squeezed them. Then he let go of her abruptly and stepped in front of her. He took off his black t-shirt and flung it behind him at her feet as he strode to the center of the room. He turned back to face her wearing only the casually sexy uniform of his tight black jeans and boots. He didn't need to command her to come to him; her body was irresistibly drawn towards his despite the fact that her brain was flashing all kinds of frightened thoughts which her body, mysteriously completely allied with her soul in those moments, bravely ignored.

"Beautiful," he said harshly as he watched her approach him, then he gripped her wrists and raised her arms straight up over her head.

The leather straps he wrapped around her wrists bound dreams with reality. She was forced to stand on tiptoe, her high-heels barely touching the floor, her bones and muscles stretched taut against her vulnerably soft skin. "What are you going to do, John?" she asked in a small voice.

"I'm going to whip you, Sofia."

"Oh, no please!" She stared helplessly at his broad shoulders and the long, straight line of his back as he moved away from her again. "I've never been whipped before, John, I don't know if-"

"I know you haven't, but it's obvious you want to be." He returned holding the long, snaking instrument she dreaded and inexplicably desired all in the same heartbeat. "For example, how many times have you called me John since you arrived?"

"But-"

"That night out in the field when you asked me if you should just call me 'my lord', I knew you were the one." He draped the whip over her shoulder so it hung down her back, and then slowly snaked it down between her breasts, letting her get a feel for how thin and firm the finely knotted leather was. "But this evening you've been addressing me as John because you think it's safer. You seem to think you can control what happens to you, that you can choose what I do or don't do to you by what you call me. You're treating me like Pavlov's dog, Sofia, imagining that if you say "John" I'll behave, and that if you say "my lord" you'll be giving me permission to attack you, as if it I needed your permission for anything."

"No!" she breathed, staring beseechingly into his eyes. "I wasn't thinking that!" Even as she said it, she knew she was only making it worse for herself by lying about it too.

He thrust the handle of the whip between her legs, pressing it against her vulva so her labial lips gaped open around the firm leather shaft. "Who am I, Sofia?"

"My lord!" she whispered.

He stepped back, inhaling the fragrance of her pussy juices coating the handle before he cracked the whip against the floor at her feet.

The sharp, loud sound it made terrified her, but only for an instant, because all that mattered was the unbelievably thrilling fact that she hadn't told him about her dream last night and yet, as if he could see into her soul, he was making it come true. He was forcing her to live what her deepest self desired. He truly *was* her lord.

Chapter Fifteen

Rhyming Reverie

On a perfectly temperate day in April,
the sun gilding showers of yellow leaves,
holding a feather-light pen indulging in reverie,
my lover splitting the wood of a dead tree,

The Fire in Starlight

I'm blessed by not feeling pressed to do anything.

Yet I can't forget trees are killed to make this paper,
the world's breath increasingly fouled by industries,
factory towers burning more cancerous cigarettes
coughing up terrible storms from the womb of the seas.
I'm just one more selfish consumer who believes
my soul and the earth are one eternally.

A drifting leaf hits me gently, silently,
its dead touch reminding me I passionately need
the satellite dish and all the pleasures of electricity.
I'd love to be free of the Grid with solar energy
but desires are fatally tangled up in affordability.

The wind picks up, blowing in gusts like my thoughts,
and a bird sings a sweet, constant note not meant for me…
It's wondrous we use microscopic organisms to brush our teeth,
Diatoms millions of years old with glass shells of intricate beauty,
like absolutely everything…

Sofia looked up from her notebook. John was setting another log on the
dead stump, balancing it with his fingertips before lifting the axe straight up
over his head with both hands. He paused there for a split second, honing
in on the grain in the wood even as his whole body rose up into the air and

he brought the weapon down with deadly force. There was a sharp crack followed by a dull thud as two perfect pieces of firewood fell off the stump onto the grass. He was replenishing her supply for next winter. When he had informed her that this particular tree was dead, it made her realize how much she needed a man like him around to help her manage the land, not to mention a house that would inevitably need repairs now and then. The dead oak was growing perilously close to her roof and hurricane season was coming. It could be dangerous living out in the woods if you didn't know what you were doing, which she certainly didn't. She had a lot to learn, and even then she wouldn't have the physical strength to chainsaw massive trunks, and then to split them up into manageable logs she could burn. She didn't like to wonder what she would do without him; merely imagining a world in which John didn't exist was so terrible and frightening that her stomach started to ache with anxiety as she tried to picture herself alone here, somehow just surviving and getting by instead of sensually relishing every second of her life.

She tore her eyes away from the sight of his strong arms and bare chest and looked back down at the poem she had written. She liked it because it expressed what she was feeling lately, the contentment and the conflicts, but she didn't really take it seriously. She was never going to be a great poet and she knew it, but that wasn't the point, in her opinion; she was just happy to be expressing herself. She put the notebook and pen down beside her on the wooden swing her sadistic lover had made for her last week and hung between two trees. She stretched her legs and rocked it gently back and forth, feasting her eyes on him again as her mind wandered...

The Fire in Starlight

Erotic pain was a fascinating thing, it was its own dimension, a vivid, powerful dream it was hard to remember afterwards when she "woke" from it. At first it had merely been a nightmare, a sensation that made everything go dark beneath its hot flash. She had not screamed beneath the whip's lashes the first time, it had been too terrible for that. She swallowed every inconceivable burst of agony silently, like an unholy communion, mysteriously digesting it. Amazingly, it wasn't long before she actually found herself craving the unbearable. He had only whipped her twice, on her first visit to his home, and then again last night, and she was very glad it was a rare event. He was wise enough to realize that such an intense experience could only happen once in a blue moon, unlike a lot of the other things they did together, some of which were nearly as violent, if not quite as excruciating.

She had been relieved, surprised, and thrilled to discover that the sinister looking wood and leather items in his root cellar were not at all torturous, on the contrary, they only intensified her pleasure by positioning her and cushioning her and holding her down in such a way that she couldn't escape it. Her favorite "toy" was a piece she thought of us a full body pew over which she knelt with her head and torso comfortably supported on soft black leather, with her wrists and ankles strapped down so she couldn't move – and had no desire to – as he used whichever one of her orifices he was in the mood for, or all three of them one after the other sometimes. She also loved the wooden cross she willingly martyred herself against as he flogged her and got her pussy so wet the only pain she felt was the absence of his cock in her cunt, and when he fucked her afterwards, time flowed mysteriously away on her juices. The first time it seemed only a matter of minutes before he climaxed and pulled out of her, but actually over half-an-hour had passed, or so he told her, she still could hardly believe it. But apparently it was indeed possible to fall into a sensual trance when her body was subjected to the stinging strokes of leather alternated by the soft caresses of a feather and the firm, moist stimulation of his kisses. The more he fucked her, the more she wanted him. The harder he was on her, the harder she wanted him to be on her. Like the forest in Spring, his predilections were growing and defining themselves, coming into their full, dark flower through her profound soul and utterly submissive body.

"Don't you need a break?" she called to him, feeling a little guilty about how hard he was working for her.

"No," he replied shortly, not even glancing over at her as he concentrated, his tanned skin gleaming like bronze mixed with pure gold in her eyes. When she first met him he was winter pale, now his goatee and black hair made her think of an ancient Persian king. There was no end to what her imagination could do with him, and in turn he couldn't seem to do enough for her physically, not just in bed but in every respect.

She picked up her pen and notebook again, but then just sat staring at her lover's flexing muscles as she struggled to understand, by somehow putting into words, why she loved being used so roughly during sex by a man who otherwise treated her with such tender respect. She had never been so happy with Steve, and maybe it was the fact that she couldn't control John that made her love him more every day. Sometimes she caught herself trying to subtly manipulate him the way she had her previous lovers, but it never worked, and how ashamed she was of herself for trying couldn't compare to how thrilled she was by the hard, inviolate core of his personality her attempts exposed. He saw right through her thoughts and actions when they weren't completely sincere, and afterwards it felt good and natural that he should punish her for being selfish and weak and continuing to indulge those parts of herself she was trying to rise above.

She gave up and got up, heading for the house to get her hardworking lover a glass of ice water. She wasn't in a place yet where she could capture in words what it felt like to be whipped, and then fucked so violently from behind that she was literally suspended on his driving erection, her wet-hot pussy a cauldron in which every sensation – the constricting strain on her wrists and arms, the burning whip marks crisscrossing her skin, his fingers digging cruelly into the tender skin of her breasts as he braced himself on them – was alchemized by the force of his thrusts into an overwhelming fulfillment that turned the conventional definition of pleasure inside out; it was a mysterious negative of pleasure the experience of which was hard to remember clearly and impossible to explain reasonably.

* * *

"What happens when your sabbatical is over, Sofia?"

She looked at him, caught off guard by the question. "I don't know." They were sitting out on his front porch again, one of their favorite places to be in the evening, the sunset an extraordinary spectacle arranged just for them. That was how she felt when she was with him – that they were the very heart of the universe. She wondered if this was the way all lovers felt.

"Are you planning to commute all the way to LSU everyday?"

"Not every day." She sipped her Chardonnay. "I'd try and schedule classes for two or three days a week only, if possible."

"Do you miss teaching?"

"Not at all!" How quickly and vehemently she replied surprised her. She hadn't consciously thought about it, but now that she did, she realized it was true – she *didn't* miss having students and papers to grade and, especially, being forced to study the same poems over and over again every year because they were a required part of the curriculum. She especially dreaded dealing with all the other teachers in the department now that Robert was gone and she wouldn't be able to hide under his wonderful, tenured wing. She would no longer have an excuse to keep to herself as much as she had when he was around, and she realized now with stomach turning clarity that she was dreading the whole cut-throat academic scene.

"Then why go back, Sofia?"

"Because I need to make a living, John." Obviously he knew that, so she couldn't understand why he would ask.

"Do you?" He looked down into his wine. The glass was perched on the buckle of his belt as he sat comfortably slouched in his chair, his right ankle resting on his left knee.

She was silent. Something immensely important was happening here, she could feel it...

"If we merged our lands, my lady," he looked up from the golden wine at the soft violet sky through the black screen, "we would own seventy acres between us. There's a lot we could do with that."

"I don't know anything about farming, John," she reminded him reluctantly, with artificial equanimity, because her heart was beating fast and hard.

"I realize that, but I know a thing or two. Besides, we'd have people for that." He smiled over at her.

"Of course!" She smiled back.

"Almost every night you trust me with your life, Sofia," he said soberly. "Trusting me with your finances is nowhere near as dangerous."

"You mean… I wouldn't need to go back to LSU?"

"Not if you don't want to."

She was silent. Even if it was only a business partnership he was proposing, it was a wonderful prospect…

"Just think about it," he concluded, sitting up and setting his wine glass down on the table.

"I don't *have* to think about it," she protested softly, staring earnestly into his eyes when he looked back at her. "I'd love to merge my land with yours, my lord. You know that…"

"Yes. Put your glass down."

She didn't smile as she obeyed him; what was between them was too intense. It wasn't just her pussy that was getting hot; her soul was threatening to burn joyfully right through her flesh as she sensed their future together being forged.

"Come here." He sat up straight and patted his lap.

She stood up and perched on his knees, relaxing against his chest as he slipped an arm over her shoulders. She caressed his chest while he stroked one of her thighs gently.

"You're beautiful," he said quietly. "I'm so happy to be here with you."

"And I'm so happy to be here with *you!*" she whispered.

"Your dreams have made my life, Sofia. Who you are, the way you are, makes it possible for me to really be myself, and I'm not just talking about our sex life. Being with you affects everything I do because of what you make me feel. Do you know what I mean?"

"Yes," she sighed, "because I feel the same way about you."

"Do you love me?"

"With all my soul, my lord!"

"And I love you. I feel as though I always have, and I believe now that I always will."

Chapter Sixteen

The forest was so green and lush, so fresh and new, it was hard to remember the skeletal branches of trees in winter. As if overnight, the oaks and maples and beech trees – and at least half a dozen other species she didn't know the names for yet – leafed out and didn't stop. The avid swiftness with which bare branches became rustling canopies made her think of little green tongues eager to taste the light, to lick the rain and kiss the breeze. John planted his spring garden – tomatoes, peppers, cucumbers, carrots, shallots and sweet onions, plus all sorts of other delicious things. He said the soil was very acidic, so he grew everything in raised beds he had made himself, naturally. He didn't use pressure-treated wood, which he considered poisonous, but a black aluminum he had found in his favorite junkyard. Her respect for him deepened with every passing day, and with every project she saw him undertake and complete with striking results.

She went to Home Depot one morning to run an errand for him. Charged with the task of finding stainless steel bolts and washers of a specific size, she came to appreciate why he sometimes spent so much time searching the isles for exactly what he needed. It took her, and two employees, almost half-an-hour to find just the right little pieces of stainless steel. Her lover built things to last, and he never rushed what he was working on; once he started something he didn't divide his concentration by initiating any other projects. In a way Sofia felt like his most special, and hopefully life-long, creative effort; she felt more relaxed and sensual than she had ever suspected was possible. She had always known she was lovely and intelligent, special in her own way, like every other human being, but there had been something roughly insecure and unfinished about her whereas now, in John's hands, her thoughts were confidently polished and her feelings glowed in a way that clearly shown in her eyes and in her smile, and even in the healthy radiance of her skin when it wasn't marked by something he had done to her.

She was perversely proud of her sensual bruises. In fact, she felt bereft when there was no evidence of his desire for her adorning her flesh.

Inside and out, emotionally and physically, she knew she was the perfect palette for him, and even though he never said as much, she sensed he felt the same way. It didn't bother her that a lot of people, especially in Louisiana, would think there was something unnatural, maybe even satanic, about their sex life. Breath-play wasn't safe; it wasn't normal. Only a devilish man could enjoy whipping the woman he loved, and she herself was a lost cause, a hopeless sinner, a true daughter of Eve and cousin to Mary Magdalene. Except that there was no evidence to support the assumption that Mary was a whore, whereas it was clearly indicated in a variety of gospels that she was Christ's most beloved disciple. The vision of history she had been force-fed was increasingly sticking in Sfoia's throat the more she read, and the more she learned about herself as she willingly submitted to the discipline of a lovingly tender yet also erotically sadistic man.

It was early May and already she had seen a black snake in her backyard. John assured her it was harmless, but she didn't get any closer to it than necessary. Spiders had also begun appearing, weaving their webs everywhere, prompting her to twist her long hair up into a baseball cap because she dreaded catching one in it, especially a big Golden Orb Weaver. The black caterpillars with the white paint splashes down their backs were gone at last busy transforming themselves into moths. In April they had been everywhere, and she had made the mistake once of laying a pair of house pants out on the back porch to finish drying. When she went out to get them there were at least fifteen caterpillars clinging to the light-green cotton they mistook for a massive leaf. She shook it out in mild disgust, not relishing the thought of future moths crawling up her crotch.

It was stunning how much more aware she was of Spring and the burgeoning of life out in the country than she ever had been in the city. At her apartment complex squirrels and a few birds lived in the trees, and of course there was no escaping the mosquitoes in summer, but that was about it as far she could remember. Certainly she had never heard, much less seen, an armadillo rooting beneath her porch. John had put an electric fence around his garden to keep out predators, three layers of wire – one close to the ground for smaller creatures, one a bit higher for armadillos and the like, and the taller one for deer. He assured her the fence gave the animals only a mild shock that deterred them from returning but didn't harm them. He offered to help her start her own garden, but she declined for the moment, not quite ready yet for so much abundance. Sometimes she needed a break from sensual stimulus and spent the whole day sitting inside at the computer, using its virtual armor to protect herself from the mysteriously demanding beauty of all the life surrounding her.

When the cows were in John's field she sat on the oak bench he had made for her and watched them. She thought of ancient Egypt and of Hathor, the goddess of love – who was often depicted as a cow with the lunar disc resting between her curved horns – and began writing another poem in her notebook...

SECRET FOREST

Little stick-um frogs on the windows at night

and sinisterly sensual moths desiring the light.

Cell-phone-faced spiders I can easily dial
the extravagant heart of all Creation on,
beautiful as gems on 3-D webs of silver thread
spun in the enchanted beam of a utility lamp.

Love-bugs always fucking without facing each other
becoming a smear of ink on my affronted flesh
as I brush off their clinging commonness.

Butterflies blue-black and Monarchs larger
than beauty so fragile should logically be
wafting right in front of me; a visual fragrance
from paradise never present long enough
except as a longing more vivid than their wings.

Humming birds fighting for plastic yellow flowers
strung out on store-bought nectar mixed with one
cup unrefined sugar, starting, stopping, plunging
into the mineral bath I filled for them because I love
their happy greedy chirping as they dip and sip;
the air subtly displaced by the unfathomable
force of wings defying reason that can't grasp
how many miraculous times they beat per second.

The Fire in Starlight

A trinity of fireflies ascended into the trees
my first night here as I rested my heavy head
on feathers buried in violet Egyptian sheets.

The moon wakes me now with its light cutting sharper
than Excalibur into fears grown thick as weeds
fighting the concrete reality in which I always lived,
depressed by cities' jaundiced skies, until these healthy
wonderful moments in time created by the true love
I always hoped to find – a squirrel running and jumping
from one branch of circumstance to another hording
the seeds of dreams, some of which fall with a clang
on the roof of my lover's workshop, rich as pharaoh's tomb
with tools for penetrating and shaping nature's beauty
around his imagination – ancient and powerful
as the black snake winding between the Ginger leaves
eating small creatures and all illusions of Eden,
a living hieroglyph consuming history
with the frightening forked tongue of countries
moving too fast crushing everything in their path.

A tuft of white and gold feathers might have been an owl
or a falcon dining on the modern road's deadly table.
The stiff bodies of delicious deer going to waste
while fat and fearful cows remain temporarily safe,

painting an ever-changing bas-relief on the landscape
teleporting me back centuries with every breath I take;
all the cells of my body magically replaced
again and again as casually as lazy jaws chew
the earth's green skin on obscenely thick tongues –
Hathor's languid priestesses passionately licking
the salt in my blood for which mosquitoes blindly risk
everything, but my goddess' hand shows them no mercy.

I caress my beloved drinking a Chardonnay
that reflects the profoundly intoxicating sunset
stretching molten fingers between the sentinel trees...
Experience bottled in precious moments labeled
with priceless conversations stored in the cellar
of the universe to open up and really enjoy
in a grave of ashes riding the wind breathing
through Love's Secret Forest...

Steve would probably accuse her of getting old and boring because one of her favorite pastimes was sitting out on her porch in the evenings sipping Chardonnay and listening to all the different birds singing. John was usually with her, and she lit candles as it got dark so he could read the small print in the bird book he consulted to figure out the names of the throats from which all the different lovely notes emanated. They spent so much time out there that they even got to know individual birds, including a male and female Cardinal who met in the same tree every evening and flew off together as night fell. She thought of all the birds that every day lost their homes when countless acres of woodland were bulldozed to make way for shopping centers, office buildings and condos. Where did they all go? For many species the answer was *nowhere*. Countless lovely songs would never be heard again, except perhaps in dreams, and in other dimensions of life that could never be destroyed.

Today, every time she touched her left shoulder blade, she suffered a sweet pain in the vulnerably soft skin that flowed up into her neck. John had fucked her from behind last night, the full weight of his body pinning hers down against the bed. He bit her as he drove into her, the sharp pressure of his teeth intensifying with his thrusts, the harder he banged her the more viciously he sucked on her. His guttural grown – in which she heard intense satisfaction combined with a dangerously growing need for even more of her – was an aphrodisiac of the most irresistible kind to Sofia. The burning pain in her neck flowed straight down into her sex like supernatural blood lubricating his hard-on and making it easier and easier for him to penetrate her as deeply as possible, then even more deeply, and deeper still. The more completely she yielded to him the more it stoked his lust, and she experienced a little of what helpless prey did in the jaws of a powerful predator – a submissive sense of peace at how desirable she was. A certain amount of pain turned her on, and it wasn't mental; it was purely and intensely physical. When he spanked her, her pussy got as hot as her ass, juicing helplessly while her blood rushed to the offended area. The tyranny of her clitoris was overthrown the minute she realized that submissively absorbing his controlled force made her sex wet like nothing else. When they spent the night together, she always had an orgasm in the morning when they made love more tenderly, but she was always thinking about the night's violent encounters as she climaxed.

The paper she was writing on the Romanian lute player songs had fallen by the wayside. She was more interested in her own poetry, inferior as it was. She also spent hours contentedly pondering the haunting power of her sex life. John could be so feral, so vicious in bed, it still amazed her how considerate and generous he was afterwards and at all other times. He was full of energy, always creating or studying or growing something. He wasn't from Louisiana, he had been raised in the mountains of Pennsylvania, but he loved East Feliciana as much as she did. "It's the perfect weather," he said, "cold enough in the winter for a fire, but it rarely snows. I got sick to death of shoveling the snow out of my parents' driveway."

"Well, I wouldn't know, I've never even seen snow. The farthest I've been is Houston, Texas for a conference."

"I'll take you to Europe, my lady. You need to travel and see the world. We'll start in Italy."

She laughed. "I'd love that, but right now I feel like I'm in a whole different world than Baton Rouge. Living out here is like an endless vacation, with responsibilities, of course," she added, "but you take care of everything for me so wonderfully, I'm more relaxed and happy than I've ever been in my life here."

"And it makes me very happy to hear you say that."

They were lying on her bed. He had just fucked her ass, and she was resting in his arms after having cleaned his cock with a warm wet washcloth, after which she used another fresh cloth to dry him off.

"I'm going to take care of you. You know that, don't you, Sofia?"

"Yes, my lord."

"My divorce will be final soon."

"I'm glad!"

"Are you?"

"Yes… I mean, I'm sorry you had to go through that, but… I'm not, really."

"You're adorably easy to tease, you know."

She sighed. "Why did you and Anne decide to move out here? If you had all that money from the sale of your company, you could have lived anywhere."

"We'd both had it with the city, and, as I said, the climate here's ideal. People think the south's hot and humid all the time. They have no idea how beautiful it can be. Louisiana has a terrible reputation for everything, that's why so much of it's still unspoiled, under-populated and affordable."

"Those *are* increasingly rare qualities," she agreed. "Most people wouldn't even know Louisiana existed if it wasn't for New Orleans, but the land and the climate are so different up here. I love them. I love *everything* about my life now."

"I'm glad." He rested his hand against her face, pressing it more firmly against his chest.

"Do you think you'll ever get bored here?" she dared to ask.

"Only boring people get bored."

She smiled. "That's true, but... you know what I mean."

"No, I don't. Why don't you tell me."

"I mean there aren't many people like us around here, John, there aren't any clubs..."

"There's one in Baton Rouge, but trust me, you wouldn't like it."

"Really? Why?"

"Let's just say most of the members aren't very decorative. They have a decent play space, with some nice toys, but when they get together on Saturday nights they mostly just sit around and talk, and believe me, the conversation isn't worth the drive."

"What do you mean they aren't *decorative*?"

"Let's just say a lot of them look like they eat too much fried pizza."

"Oh... yuck."

"Exactly."

"Then I'm essentially right, there aren't any clubs-"

"Are you thinking about your gang-bang fantasy, Sofia? It *is* going to be hard to find the right men around here for that."

"No, I'm thinking about *you*, my lord," she quickly protested, wondering if he could feel how her heart had sped up.

"What about me, my lady?"

"Have you ever been with two women at the same time?" she blurted.

"Oh, yes. Anne was bi-sexual."

"Oh... don't you miss it? I mean, is just being with me all the time enough for you?"

"No, it's not enough, it's everything. I love you, Sofia. There are experiences that, on occasion, would make our sex life exciting in a different way than it already is, but it would never be better, it would just be different, and it would be pleasurable because we'd be sharing the experience. There are lots of fantasies I'd love to live out with you, but that doesn't mean I'm not perfectly happy just being here with you now."

She sighed again. "Steve was always getting restless, and bored. He was never satisfied with anything; nothing could hold his interest for long."

"You're with me now, Sofia. Try and remember that."

"That's funny, my lord, because you're *all* I think about, *really*."

"Well, I hope you can spare a thought for dinner, because I'm starving."

"It's already on the stove, ready whenever we are… Why do you think I have a gang-bang fantasy?"

"You forget I've read your dreams. There are always other men around, and not just one or two, but a whole crowd of handsome men wearing black leather. I know what you'd like more than anything, trust me."

"But those were just dreams…"

"Excuse me?"

"Forgive me, my lord." He shouldn't need to remind her that she had first seen the man she loved and in whose arms she was lying now in *just* a dream.

Chapter Seventeen

I t was a glorious morning. After days of rain and brooding clouds and being trapped indoors, Sofia abandoned her chores and escaped into the forest. She knew which path to take, the one that led towards the place where they had met one evening and gazed up at the moon and the stars together. She would never forget the feel of his warm, heavy arm around her as he walked her back to her fireside, and how she could not wait to give herself to him, body and soul. She knew she would be his wife one day, she just didn't know when, and she prayed the breeze caressing her uncovered hair would fly to his window today and whisper of her longing to see him again in their secret place, where he first took her in his arms and kissed her lips.

All the leaves were wet, forming halos of soft green light sparkling with stars as the sun ascended between the trees, burning away the mist wrapped thick as furs around the noble old trees. The morning was chilly but she walked quickly, and soon she not only felt warm but happier than she knew she should be in an evil world full of suffering. Yet the birds were chirping joyfully, their songs ringing through the otherwise silent woods blessedly drowning out all doubts about the future so that it seemed to stretch before her as beautifully as the day. Birds were ruthless warriors in the eyes of bugs and worms armed with the swords of their beaks and cloaked in divine feathers. Their enchanting notes weren't meant for her, yet they filled her with hope, as though their music was sung directly into God's ear and humans just happened to overhear.

Her heart took off in her breast, urging her feet to run faster across the grass when she reached the end of the path leading out into the clearing where she had met him that evening. The sky was impossibly far away, a delicate blue bowl knocked upside down during the battle between good and evil from which the world spilled forth, and in which her soul was only a drop of trembling water reflecting the light of eternity in her thoughts. There was not a single cloud in the heavenly dome. If there truly were angels they were lazily lounging somewhere else today on their infinitely soft beds. She stopped in the middle of the meadow to catch her breath, and her hopes, which had gotten away from her, and left her feeling more alone than ever because he was not there.

A shadow swept across the grass before her, startling her into glancing over her shoulder as if Death had touched her. She looked up and saw a falcon soaring overhead, its wings fully spread. She took an exultant breath, and it was then that she saw him emerge from beneath the trees on the opposite side of the meadow.

She ran as fast as a rabbit terrified by the bird of prey circling overhead, but in truth she was hurrying towards him because her life depended on it.

He waited for her at the edge of the forest, and lifted her off her feet as he caught her in his arms. "Sofia!" he whispered.

"My lord!" she breathed. "I knew you would be here! I *prayed* you would be!"

"And I heard your prayers, for the whole world speaks to me with your voice, my love."

"And you, my lord, mean more to me than God!"

"Never say that, Sofia." He set her down and gripped her firmly by the arms as he stared down into her eyes. "Look at me. I am only a man."

"No, you are the sun, without which I would be nothing, my soul only darkness and longing for you, my Lord!"

He pulled her roughly against him and kissed her, forcing her mouth open beneath his, and even though their tongues spoke silently of worms in the grave, she knew their love would defy death.

*From The Bard of the Dimbovitza – Romanian Folk Songs Collected From The Peasants by Helene Vacaresco, translated by Carmen Sylva and Alma Strettell, London and New York Harper & Brothers, 1914

Maria Isabel Pita is the author of three BDSM Erotic Romances – *Thorsday Night, Eternal Bondage* and *To Her Master Born*, re-printed as an exclusive hard-cover edition by the Doubleday Venus Book Club. She is the author of two Paranormal Erotic Romances *Dreams of Anubis* and *Rituals of Surrender*, and of three Contemporary Erotic Romances *A Brush With Love, Recipe For Romance*, and *Cat's Collar*. Maria has also written two non-fiction books, *The Story of M – A Memoir* and *Beauty & Submission*, and a book of erotic stories set all through history entitled *Guilty Pleasures*. All of Maria's books have been Doubleday Venus Book Club selections. You can visit her at www.mariaisabelpita.com

Announcing the EAA *Signature*
and Print On Demand Erotic

Help support the Erotic Authors Association as well as your favorite erotica authors! Some of our most prestigious members have given the EAA exclusive rights to publish their newest or most popular erotic books. Most titles are available as ebooks as well as print on

---

Support quality erotica!
Buy our books!
Stroke your brain!

Series Erotic Ebooks Trade Paperbacks!

demand books and are frequently not available for sale anywhere else. A portion of the proceeds helps support the EAA and its mission to promote quality erotica writing and publishing around the world. New authors are added every month so be sure to visit often!

---

www.eroticauthorsassociation.com

**Marilyn Jaye Lewis,
Founder and Executive Director**

Magic Carpet Books

Catalogue

The Collector's Edition of the Lost Erotic Novels

Edited by
Major LaCaritilie

Fiction/Erotica
ISBN 0-97553317-7
Trade Paperback 5-3/16"x 8"
608 Pages
$16.95 ($22.95 Canada)

MISFORTUNES OF MARY – Anonymous, 1860's:

An innocent young woman who still believes in the kindness of strangers unwittingly signs her life away to a gentleman who makes demands upon her she never would have dreamed possible.

WHITE STAINS – Anaïs Nin & Friends, 1940's:

Sensual stories penned by Anaïs and some of her friends that were commissioned by a wealthy buyer for $1.00 a page. These classics of pornography are not included in her two famous collections, *Delta of Venus* and *Little Birds*.

INNOCENCE – Harriet Daimler, 1950's:

A lovely young bed-ridden woman would appear to be helpless and at the mercy of all around her, and indeed, they all take advantage of her in shocking ways, but who's to say she isn't the one secretly dominating them?

THE INSTRUMENTS OF THE PASSION – Anonymous, 1960's:

A beautiful young woman discovers that there is much more to life in a monastery than anyone imagines as she endures increasingly intense rituals of flagellation devotedly visited upon her by the sadistic brothers.

The Collector's Edition of Victorian Erotica

Edited by
Major LaCaritilie

Fiction/Erotica

ISBN 0-9755331-0-X

Trade Paperback · 5-3/16"x 8"

608 Pages

$15.95 ($18.95 Canada)

No lone soul can possibly read the thousands of erotic books, pamphlets and broadsides the English reading public were offered in the 19th century. It can only be hoped that this Anthology may stimulate the reader into further adventures in erotica and its manifest reading pleasure. In this unique anthology, 'erotica' is a comprehensive term for bawdy, obscene, salacious, pornographic and ribald works including, indeed featuring, humour and satire that employ sexual elements. Flagellation and sadomasochism are recurring themes. They are activities whose effect can be shocking, but whose occurrence pervades our selections, most often in the context of love and affection. This anthology includes selections from such Anonymous classics as *A Weekend Visit, The Modern Eveline, Misfortunes of Mary, My Secret Life, The Man With A Maid, The Life of Fanny Hill, The Mournings of a Courtesan, The Romance of Lust, Pauline, Forbidden Fruit* and *Venus School-Mistress.*

The Collector's Edition of Victorian Lesbian Erotica

Edited By Major LaCaritilie

Fiction/Erotica

ISBN 0-9755331-9-3

Trade Paperback · 5 3/16 x 8 608 Pages

$17.95 ($24.95Canada)

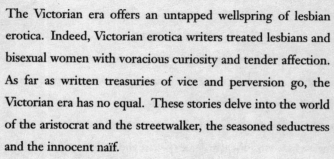

The Victorian era offers an untapped wellspring of lesbian erotica. Indeed, Victorian erotica writers treated lesbians and bisexual women with voracious curiosity and tender affection. As far as written treasuries of vice and perversion go, the Victorian era has no equal. These stories delve into the world of the aristocrat and the streetwalker, the seasoned seductress and the innocent naïf.

Represented in this anthology are a variety of genres, from romantic fiction to faux journalism and travelogue, as well as styles and tones resembling everything from steamy page-turners to scholarly exposition. What all these works share, however, is the sense of fun, mischief and sexiness that characterized Victorian lesbian erotica.

The lesbian erotica of the Victorian era defies stereotype and offers rich portraits of a sexuality driven underground by repressive mores. As Oscar Wilde claimed, the only way to get rid of temptation is to yield to it.

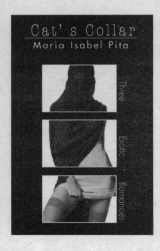

Cat's Collar –
Three Erotic Romances

By Maria Isabel Pita

Fiction/Erotica
ISBN 0-9766510-0-9
Trade Paperback · 5 3/16 x 8
608 Pages
$16.95 ($ 20.95 Canada)

Dreams of Anubis

A legal secretary from Boston visiting Egypt explores much more than just tombs and temples in the stimulating arms of Egyptologist Simon Taylor. But at the same time a powerfully erotic priest of Anubis enters her dreams, and then her life one night in the dark heart of Cairo's timeless bazaar. Sir Richard Ashley believes he has lived before and that for centuries he and Mary have longed to find each other again. Mary is torn between two men who both desire to discover the legendary tomb of Imhotep and win the treasure of her heart.

Rituals of Surrender

All her life Maia Wilson has lived near a group of standing stones in the English countryside, but it isn't until an old oak tree hit by lightning collapses across her car one night that she suddenly finds herself the heart of an erotic web spun by three sexy, enig-matic men - modern Druids intent on using Maia for a dark and ancient rite...

Cat's Collar

Interior designer Mira Rosemond finds herself in one attractive successful man's bedroom after the other, but then one beautiful morning a stranger dressed in black leather takes a short cut through her garden and changes the course of her life forever. Mira has never met anyone quite like Phillip, and the more she learns about his mysterious profession - secretly linked to some of Washington's most powerful women - the more frightened and yet excited she becomes as she finds herself falling helplessly, submissively in love.

Praise for Maria Isabel Pita...

Dreams of Anubis is a compellingly erotic tale unveiled in one of the world's most romantic and mystical lands... Ms. Pita brings together both a sensually historic plot and a contemporary Egypt... her elegant style of writing pulls at your senses and allows you to live the moment through her characters. The language flows beautifully, the characters are well drawn, the plot is exciting and always fresh and riveting, and the setting is romantic. I highly recommend Dreams of Anubis for anyone with a love of erotic romance with a touch of magic and mysticism. —*Just Erotic Romance Reviews*

Maria Isabel Pita is already one of the brightest stars in the erotic romance genre. If you're unfamiliar with her work, she specializes in transporting her readers effortlessly between the past and present, while indestructible true love weaves its eternal spell on her characters' minds and souls. —*Marilyn Jaye Lewis*

The Story of M – A Memoir

by Maria Isabel Pita

Non-Fiction/Erotica • ISBN 0-9726339-5-2

Trade Paperback · 5 3/16 x 8 · 239 Pages •

$14.95 ($18.95 Canada)

The true, vividly detailed and profoundly erotic account of a beautiful, intelligent woman's first year of training as a slave to the man of her dreams.

Maria Isabel Pita refuses to fall into any politically correct category. She is not a feminist, and yet she is fiercely independent. She is everything but a mindless sex object, yet she is willingly, and happily, a masterful man's love slave. M is erotically submissive and yet also profoundly secure in herself, and she wrote this account of her ascent into submission for all the women out there who might be confused and frightened by their own contradictory desires just as she was.

M is the true highly erotic account of the author's first profoundly instructive year with the man of her dreams. Her vividly detailed story makes it clear we should never feel guilty about daring to make our deepest, darkest longings come true, and serves as living proof that they do.

Beauty & Submission

by Maria Isabel Pita

Non-Fiction/Erotica •
ISBN 0-9755331-1-8
Trade Paperback ·
5-3/16" x 8" · 256 Pages
$14.95 ($18.95 Canada)

In a desire to tell the truth and dispel negative stereotypes about the life of a sex slave, Maria Isabel Pita wrote *The Story of M... A Memoir*. Her intensely erotic life with the man of her dreams continues now in *Beauty & Submission*, a vividly detailed sexual and philosophical account of her second year of training as a slave to her Master and soul mate.

"A sex slave is very often a woman who dares to admit to herself exactly what she wants. Absolute submission to love requires a mysterious strength of character that is a far cry from the stereotype of sex slaves as mindless doormats with no self-respect. Before I entered the BDSM lifestyle with the man I now call "my Master" as casually as other women say "my husband" I did not believe a sex slave could lead a normal, healthy life. I thought my dreams of true love and my desire for a demanding Master were like matter and anti-matter canceling each other out. I have since learned otherwise, and Beauty & Submission continues the detailed account of my ascent into submission as an intelligent woman with an independent spirit who is now also willingly and happily a masterful man's love slave." —*From Beauty & Submission*

Guilty Pleasures

by Maria Isabel Pita

Fiction/Erotica

ISBN 0-9755331-5-0

Trade Paperback · 5 3/16 x 8 · 304 Pages ·

$16.95 ($21.95 Canada)

Guilty Pleasures explores the passionate willingness of women throughout the ages to offer themselves up to the forces of love. Historical facts are seamlessly woven into intensely graphic sexual encounters beginning with ancient Egypt and journeying down through the centuries to the present and beyond. Beneath the covers of Guilty Pleasures you will find eighteen erotic love stories with a profound feel for the times and places where they occur. An ancient Egyptian princess… a courtesan rising to fame in Athen's Golden Age… a widow in 15th century Florence initiated into a Secret Society… a Transylvanian Count's wicked bride… an innocent nun tempted to sin in 17th century Lisbon… a lovely young woman finding love in the Sultan's harem… and many more are all one eternal woman in Guilty Pleasures.

Select Reviews:

'*Guilty Pleasures*' is a collection of eighteen erotic short stories. These stories take you on an erotic journey through time, each one taking you further back in time than the story before it, until there is no time at all. Maria Isabel Pita is an imaginative writer with a skill for writing beautiful prose. She has taken her love for history to create a collection of stories that makes you want to keep reading. Her heroines are strong and the tales told from their point of view pull you in and make you want to know more about their individual stories. The author's attention to detail and historical accuracy makes it easier for the reader to fall into the stories as they read. This collection has something for everyone. I would highly recommend this collection of short stories. There is nothing guilty about the pleasure received from reading it. —*Romance Divas*

Pita does indeed take us through the ages, from the near-future time of 2015 A.D., back through the 20th century, then the 19th, 18th, 17th, 16th, 15th, 12th centuries, back to 1000 B.C., 3000 B.C., through to another solar system, and on to a parallel universe. What will amaze you, if not even alarm you, is Pita's eye for detail and her uncanny feel for the everyday lives of her distant characters. When you read her stories of ancient lovers, for example, you will believe that Pita herself has visited those times and is merely recounting to you first-hand what she observed, endured, and felt while she was there. The storytelling is seamless and flowing. The erotic encounters between her characters are sexually explicit and arousing, sometimes emotionally raw, and often thought-provoking for the reader. Pita's unique imagination is unleashed and she spares no punches. *Guilty Pleasures* is an absolute must for any fan of literary erotica.

Marilyn Jaye Lewis – Erotic Author's Association Review

A Brush With Love
by Maria Isabel Pita

Non-Fiction/Erotica
ISBN 0-9774311-1-8
Trade Paperback · 5 3/16 x 8
254 Pages · $12.95

The cobbled streets of Boston wind back into a past full of revolutionary fervor and stretch passionately into the future inside the thoughts and desires of Miranda Covington, a young and beautiful professional artist's model.

Michael Keneen knows exactly what he wants to do in life, even if it means disappointing his parents by not continuing a tradition of three generations in law enforcement. For Michael, artist models are only aesthetic challenges on the path to his Master in Fine Arts, until one freezing December afternoon Miranda Covington takes the stand, then suddenly getting her beauty down on paper isn't all he wants to do.

Lost in hot daydreams that often become reality when she poses for handsome clients in private, Miranda doesn't notice the sea of faces around her while she poses, until Patrick's penetrating blue eyes meet hers. He might not be a cop like his father, but his arresting personality is irresistible, especially when he discovers hidden longings in Miranda that challenge all her conventional ideas about love in ways that excite her like nothing ever has...

My Secret Fantasies –
Sixty Erotic Love Stories

ISBN: 0-9755331-2-6

$11.95 U.S. / 16.95 Canada

In My Secret Fantasies, sixty different women share the secret of how they made their wildest erotic desires come true. Next time you feel like getting your heart rate up and your blood really flowing, curl up with a cup of tea and *My Secret Fantasies...*

The Ties That Bind

By Vanessa Duriés

Non-Fiction/Erotica ISBN 0-9766510-1-7
Trade Paperback5 3/16 x 8
160 Pages$14.95 ($18.95 Canada)

RE-PRINT OF THE FRENCH BEST-SELLER: The incredible confessions of a thrillingly unconventional woman. From the first page, this chronicle of dominance and submission will keep you gasping with its vivid depicitons of sensual abandon. At the hand of Masters Georges, Patrick, Pierre and others, this submissive seductress experiences pleasures she never knew existed...

"I am not sentimental, yet I love my Master and do not hide the fact. He is everything that is intelligent, charming and strict. Of course, like every self-respecting master, he sometimes appears very demanding, which pains and irritates me when he pushes me to the limits of my moral and physical resistance. My Master is impassioned, and he lives only for his passion: sadomasochism. This philosophy, for it is one, represents in his eyes an ideal way of life, but I am resolutely opposed to that view. One cannot, one must not be a sadomasochist the whole time. The grandeurs and constraints of everyday life do not live happily with fantasies. One must know how to protect one from the other by separating them openly. When the master and the slave live together, they must have the wisdom to alternate the sufferings and the languors, the delights and the torments...."

Secret Desires: Two Erotic Romances

ISBN: 0-9766510-7-6
$12.95

DIGGING UP DESTINY by Frances LaGatta: Atop Machu Picchu - lost Inca City in the Clouds - archeology professor Blake Sevenson unearths a sealed cave marked by a golden sun god. Behind that stone wall resides a priceless ransom of gold and silver. Hope Burnsmyrehas has a brand new PhD, no field experience, and high hopes. She and Blake clash at every turn, but the chemistry between them makes the jungle feel even hotter.

DREAMS & DESIRES by Laura Muir:

Poet Isabel Taylor buys a stack of magazines for inspiration, and discovers the man of her dreams staring back at her from a glossy full-page electric guitar ad. That night she has a vivid encounter with Alex Goodman in her dreams, and when his band comes to town she joins a crowd of groupies backstage. When he whispers, 'Don't I know you?' the first thrilling note is struck in a romantic tour-de-force in which their desire challenges all rational limits...

MAGIC CARPET BOOKS

Order Form

Name: _____

Address: _____

City: _____

State:_____ Zip:_____

Title	ISBN	Quantity

Send check or money order to:

Magic Carpet Books
PO Box 473
New Milford, CT 06776

Postage free in the United States add $2.50 for
packages outside the United States

magiccarpetbooks@earthlink.net

Visit our website at:
www.magic-carpet-books.com